PARIS PERFECT

A novella

BY
JUNE E. RIVES

Copyright © 2017 June E. Rives
All rights reserved
First Edition

Fulton Books, Inc.
Meadville, PA

First originally published by Fulton Books 2017

ISBN 978-1-63338-537-5 (Paperback)
ISBN 978-1-63338-538-2 (Digital)

Printed in the United States of America

À Christian qui commence tous.

CHAPTER 1

A Penny for Punkin Lowery

Paris, September 10, 2000

"There it was, on the carpet outside my hotel room door. It was a sous or in English, a penny. My mother told me if you find a penny, an angel is looking out for you. I hope that is true. I am scared to death about this move, but it is great to be back in Paris, the land of gentle people who know how to enjoy life.
Writing in this journal keeps me sane after the year I've had. I am moving into my new apartment today that overlooks the Eiffel Tower. The city smells like perfume and rain."

Punkin Lowery had indeed had a horrible year. Before her arrival in Paris on this Fall day, her fiancé had committed suicide, her mother had died of cancer and the business that defined her had failed. She was turning 50 in a few months, and felt old. Having nothing to lose, she decided to move to the place she loved the most in the world- Paris. She had loved it since she first visited at 16. She even majored in French in college. Living in the South, in Houston, there was not much opportunity to speak the language, but she had pursued French clients for her advertising business. There were so many French- based companies in oil-rich Houston.

Punkin was a fifth generation Texan with a lingering pioneer spirit. She was 6 feet tall in her "stocking feet" as the old Southern expression goes, with mesmerizing green eyes. They seemed almost iridescent at times. Her best asset, they could transform into a deep violet with a change of wardrobe or mood. She was very proud, too, of her long blonde hair which dipped in waves and curls framing her face, a perfect oval.

She didn't find Alex, thank goodness. She got a call from his best friend Mike who shared a house with him. Apparently Alex had gone to his office, put a shotgun in his mouth and pulled the trigger. He left a cryptic note that explained nothing.

Shortly after his death, Punkin, and his mother, Louise, went to Alex's apartment in an elegant high rise near Memorial Park. It was neat as a pin. It looked as if Alex was coming right back. The dining room table was elegantly set. He did love to entertain. She slipped away, and went into the bedroom. She opened his jewelry box on the Chippendale chest of drawers, and took out an Italian silver chain he always wore. She put it on, hiding it under her blouse.

In his closet she found his kimono robe. She took that, too. It still smelled of Alex. The funeral had been gruesome. Of course it was a closed casket. His mother actually said to Punkin that if she and Alex had married, he would not have died. This was a pretty big guilt trip. It precipitated her going into therapy, and beginning massive journal writing.

It was just three months to the day of Alex's death that her dear mother, Big Punkin, died of an aggressive cancer. In the last weeks of her mother's life, Punkin had become the parent and her mother the child. Big P would look at "Little P" with the desperate eyes of the terminally ill. Those eyes said I want to go, but do not want to leave you.

Punkin's plans to move and totally change her life kept her alive. That, and the love and friendship of The Birthday Club. She had known these girls since kindergarten. All of them had married and had children. Punkin was the only one terminally single. She kind of felt left out of the club.

"Miss Punkin" had been spoiled all her life. She was the only child of indulgent, wealthy parents, and the apple of her father's eye. He called her his "Dreamboat". Whatever Punkin wanted, she got. She had no concept of the importance of money because it had always been there. She remembered as a child thinking how cool it was to just sign a "chit" at the country club for anything she wanted. Her naivete was coming back to bite her in the butt. Bills were piling up, and in this year of 2000, the beginning of a new century, stock markets were crashing, and there was no new business to be had.

Life changed quickly for her at 18. "Big T", her father had run off with his very young secretary, leaving Punkin with major abandonment issues. She and her mother had been left well-fixed, but she missed her father desperately. Punkin was a bit neurotic, self-centered, and anxious, but she was a friendly girl with a bright smile, which showed off her dimples. She had a most raucous laugh, and a loud singing voice.

Punkin was smart and inherited her father's acumen for business. For years her business had prospered. Her fluency in French had added to her success. Her career had become her life. The years passed quickly, but she was still alone.

She was not successful in the love department. At 25, her first fiancé, Andrew, left her at the altar. He married someone else two months later. After Andrew, there was Christopher who just wanted a mother. Then came William, recently divorced. Punkin was his "transitional woman". Finally, right before she met Alex, she had a stupid affair with a married friend of her father's.

Alex appeared as the proverbial "knight in shining armor". Most Texas men bored Punkin, but he was an exception, really more European in nature. A prominent architect, 10 years Punkin's senior, he had studied at the *Ecole des Beaux Arts* in Paris. He loved Paris as much as she did. They had that in common plus a love of backgammon, good books, great wine, and conversation. They talked often about moving to Paris after they married.

Alex had designed some of the grandest buildings in Houston. He had been a confirmed bachelor until he laid eyes on Punkin. They had been dating about a six months when they got engaged. Punkin began to notice a kind of softness and femininity about him. She thought it odd that he and Mike shared a house at their ages. She tried to ignore it. She was finally getting married and becoming a member of the club. Plus, the sex was ok, so she let this emotional twinge pass.

Life in stifling Texas was unbearable. Other Americans had been escaping to Europe for centuries. This was her chance. But first, she had to deal with death again. Today was her mother's funeral.

CHAPTER 2

The Funeral

"Dear God, help me through this day. How I will ever get along without my mother? She was my best friend and I dream about her all the time. In my dreams she is so real and I can touch her. I am blessed that I was with her at the end. I do believe in the spirit world. She didn't go until she was ready. I saw her bat away at the air one time a few weeks before she passed. I think it was an angel saying 'come on', but she was not having any of it yet.

I hope my grief doesn't make me do a stupid thing like I did after Alex died. Had sex with an old boyfriend. I was crazed and didn't know what to do. I am pretty crazed right now, really on the edge.

Thank God for my dearest friends. Kathy will be here shortly to pick me up and then we are all having lunch after the service. Maybe a martini will help me choke down the food."

It was a blazing hot Texas day, an August scorcher that the Lone Star State is famous for. Punkin hated Texas summers with their encompassing heat and humidity. She felt constipated by the weather and her life. Her emotions were swinging wildly between bouts of crying and hysterical laughter. Both these emotions came out of nowhere.

Her mother had a heart as big as Texas. Everyone said Punkin favored her in both looks and personality. The "never say die" Big P had tried chemotherapy as a last resort. After each treatment, she told Punkin she just wanted to die. There was a brief couple of weeks when the chemo seemed to be working, but it was too little, too late.

The memory was fresh in her mind of her mother's last night when she couldn't sleep and the two talked through the night.

The funeral was at 11am. Punkin was sitting in her *Pierre Deux* designed kitchen needlepointing like Madame Lafarge in Dicken's *A Tale of Two Cities*. In times of stress, keeping her hands occupied calmed her. On the kitchen table, next to stacks of Julia Child cookbooks, were a mountain of bills. A notice in big black letters said her office would be closed if the rent wasn't paid. She hadn't paid her few loyal employees who had stayed with her either. At her feet, seeming a little agitated as well, was her precious wire- haired terrier, Maurice. He never left her side. Loving and taking care of him took her mind off her troubles.

She had a big task today. To say goodbye to the best mother a girl could have. She headed to her bedroom to put on a tasteful Brooks Brothers sheath, and her mother's pearls. She arranged her hair in a chignon, and piled on the red lipstick. Her best friend, Kathy, was picking her up for the graveside service. Kathy was her oldest friend, and a charter member of The Birthday Club. People said they looked like sisters.

She arrived at Punkin's palatial town home in River Oaks, the most expensive enclave in Houston, around 10:30, giving them plenty of time to get to the cemetery. She enveloped Punkin in her arms, and Punkin dissolved into tears. With strong arms, Kathy assisted her to the car. They got to the cemetery in record time, this being a Saturday. The horrible traffic of Houston diminished somewhat on the weekends. A large crowd of both Punkin and Big P's friends was already assembled. Seeing them threw Punkin into a panic. She started twisting her mother's pearls like worry beads. She grabbed Kathy's arm in a deathlike grip.

"What a nightmare! Alex is gone, and Big P is gone, and I wake up in a cold sweat every night. I am so totally broke."

Kathy felt deeply for her oldest friend. On the money issue, she knew Punkin had seen the warning signs months before. The death of her two most precious loved ones came without warning. Kathy had experienced her own trials and tribulations in life, and Punkin had always been there for her. Punkin helped her make the biggest decision of her life- to marry the right guy instead of the wrong one. Kathy released herself from Punkin's grip with much difficulty. Punkin was holding on so hard, that little red welts were still showing on Kathy's arm.

"Dear P, this is all so heartbreaking losing both Big P and Alex at the same time. And your business. it was your whole life besides those two."

She kissed Kathy, and said in a voice, raspy with crying, and no louder than a whisper.

"Wasn't Big P the grandest lady? She was always the life of the party. We joked often that she wanted my life and I wanted hers. I guess life, like a fortune cookie, never gives you the wish you want."

Steam heat rose from the asphalt in the cemetery driveway. The sturdy crepe myrtles, flowers Punkin detested, were even wilting in the heat. The minister, sweating under his robes, gave a lovely service. He had known the family well. He reminded all of Big P's vibrant spirit, love of life and unending generosity. He ended the service with his benediction.

"We commend today, oh Lord, our dear friend and mother, Big Punkin Lowery, to your loving care."

Punkin felt she could not breathe. She hoped she didn't throw up. The heat and grief were choking her. As the service ended, all rallied round with comforting condolences. Punkin was relieved it was over. She and Kathy were off to meet The Birthday Club for lunch at the country club.

CHAPTER 3

The Birthday Club

Driving along Allen Parkway, a beautiful winding road along Buffalo Bayou into downtown, they came upon a large pear tree on the banks of the bayou. Kathy pulled over and stopped the car. She knew this was a special place for Punkin. The tree had been planted in memory of Alex. They walked over to the tree glistening in the sun.

"That was such a beautiful dedication. Even the mayor attended. Have you seen much of Alex's mother since?" Kathy asked as she held Punkin's hand

"No, but she all I have left of Alex. My therapist says that her asinine comment about my preventing his death by marrying him was just her way of grieving."

"So sad. I believe suicide is life's most selfish act. Once the decision is made, no one can stop it. I hate to remind you, that 'Les girls' told you Alex was trouble. We heard lots of rumors about him and Mike."

Punkin wanted to lash out at her friend, but she held her tongue. Hindsight is 20/20 as the old saw goes.

"I know. Shame on me. I feel a fool. Too bad when one is in love, reason goes out the window. WHY is that?"

"Beats the hell out of me," stoic Kathy shrugged as they walked back to the car.

"Les girls will certainly want to know what your next move is. You haven't even told me. What ARE you going to be when you grow up?"

PARIS PERFECT

Punkin steeled herself up to her full 6 feet in the car seat and said in a rush of words,

"Big P left me 100,000 dollars and I will get about 50,000 dollars from the sale of my business. Once I settle my debts, that should leave me enough to live in Paris for a year."

"Wow, what a decision, but I say bravo!"

Kathy knew Punkin was wild about Paris.

Besides the worrisome sexuality of Alex, the Birthday Club all knew about Punkin's financial troubles. If you grew up in Houston, especially in their social set, it was a small town. Kathy hoped none of their friends would bring up any sordid details. Some of these lifelong friends were a little jealous of Punkin and her independence.

They pulled up into the driveway of the country club, a large anti-bellum style building with majestic white columns and a sweeping front porch. It was an oasis in the urban sprawl. Centuries old pecan and magnolia trees gave the building cooling shade in the always sweltering weather.

The valet took the car. They entered the expansive entry hall, continuing into the dining room where the other girls were already seated. The room was decorated in an Old South style with painted silk paneling on the walls depicting scenes from plantation life. Large windows gave out onto a grand terrace that looked over the golf course. Houston was always hot, but it was also lush with vegetation. The magnolia trees gave off a heady fragrance through the terrace doors.

The Birthday Club was a varied bunch. Kathy was blonde like Punkin and they had been college roommates. She was happily married and had two almost-grown children. Next, there was Punkin's nearly oldest friend, Margaret. Their parents had been in each other's weddings, and the girls were only three months apart in age. She was kind of plump, having inherited that from her mother. She had beautiful auburn hair and a peaches and cream complexion. Her first husband had deserted her and their baby daughter and the pain still lingered. She was now married to a fabulous guy with whom she had a second child, a son. Both she and her second husband doted on the two children.

The third member of the group was Janey. She was a good old girl with an infectious smile. She always looked like she had just heard a joke. She was the girls' cheerleader and had a positive word for every situation. Janey had married young, right out of high school, and immediately started having children. There was five in all, so far. Her husband was a wonderful man, but not very successful. They were struggling to keep up with the others in this upper class strata.

Rounding out the group was Merry. She was the most recent addition to the Club having met the girls in first grade. She was pencil thin with prematurely gray hair. Her narrow pinched face and thin lips matched her sour attitude. She was married to the richest and most conservative man in this group. She had the annoying habit of constantly quoting his opinion. She had strong opinions, too, and was constantly mouthing off.

Each girl had a word as Punkin reached the table.

"Heh, Popo, we love ya girl," said Margaret

Janey got up from the table to give her a big bear hug.

"I second that emotion. We are all so sorry. I hope you can stay for a long lunch."

Merry, who did not get up from the table said,

"Not sure I can stay for a long lunch, but the service for your mom was lovely."

Punkin gazed around the table at her oldest and dearest friends. She felt warmth in her heart, even for sour-puss Merry. The heat and emotion of the day had worn her down. She needed a big drink.

"Who wants a martini?"

"Good idea," Margaret said

"I never drink at lunch", Merry said through tight lips.

"Well, it is 5 o'clock somewhere", party girl Janey added

"I always love a glass of something at lunch- so French." Kathy said, and winked at Punkin.

Lilly, the dining room waitress, brought their drinks on a silver tray. In this southern city, most of the help at the country club were black. To their credit, most of the girls, except for Merry, always treated Lilly and the others as friends, not hired help.

Punkin began her discourse on her Paris plans. The martini was going right to her head and she felt ebullient and excited. The group let out a collective gasp at the news. Then all started advising Punkin what to do. Kathy was first.

"Ah Paris, I do love it so! You go girl!"

"Oh Katrine, how can you say that? Those people just do not like us. And after we saved their asses in WW2."

Margaret said this as if smelling something bad.

"I agree. I call them the 'cheese-eaters'," said well-poisoner Merry

"Good one, Merr." Margaret chuckled

Since Merry had some validation, she continued.

"And you know you cannot drink their water or use their toilet paper. Bobby always makes me carry a few rolls when we go out of the good 'ole US of A."

Janey quickly tried to get the conversation back on a more positive note.

"Have you found a place to live? I understand Paris has some beautiful buildings".

Punkin could have kissed her.

"Yes, the most fabulous place with a stunning view of the Eiffel Tower. My cousin Richard calls the Tower, 'Santa Rita Number One'".

All the girls laughed at Punkin's joke. Being from oil-rich Texas, the Eiffel Tower did look like an oil derrick.

Punkin pulled out her cell phone and passed it around the table, so all the girls could see pictures of the apartment.

"What a view! This picture looks like the Tower is actually rising out of your living room windows." Janey was quite impressed.

"And the apartment looks huge. How many bedrooms, and when can I come visit?" Kathy said

"It has two bedrooms and two baths and is 1500 square feet. More space than I need, and a little over my budget, but I could not resist after seeing the view."

Then to be a little mean, she added,

"And Merry, I will certainly stock up on American toilet paper before I go"

Talking about France got the girls reminiscing about their high school French teacher, Guillaume.

"Remember what a hunk Monsieur Petit was? Maybe you can find someone like that over there," said Margaret.

"Yeah, you know what they say. Better to learn a language in 'pillow talk'". Janey said with a sly grin.

"We know you love the language and everything French. Naming your dog Maurice after Maurice Chevalier was so cute", said Kathy

The easy conversation, plus the martinis, now in their second serving, put Punkin in a very convivial mood.

"Didn't you love my Christmas card last year with me in my feather boa, and Maurice in his bowler hat?"

What a difference a few months make, Punkin thought to herself. Christmas was when Alex had proposed.

"That was so clever. I understand the French are just wild about their dogs. Maybe Maurice can help you make some new friends," said Janey

Meanwhile, Merry was watching all the attention that Punkin was getting. Since no one was paying attention to her, she switched gears.

"Oh look at the time. We should order. I have carpool this afternoon."

CHAPTER 4

Moving On

"One more session today with Dr. B. I am tired of talking about Alex, my mother, and my so-called neurosis. I am not that difference from most people, am I? Just a few more weeks and I will be out of this 'burg. I really hate this town. I love my friends but there has got to be a better life out there somewhere. At least the business has sold and I have found some renters for the house, although I do not really care if I ever see this place again either. I never really liked this house, but it was a good investment. Why do I always have to worry about money?"

The weeks until Punkin's departure were a blur. She did indeed sell her firm for a reasonable price. Her reputation in the business was still worth something. It felt good to get out of debt temporarily. She leased her townhouse to some oil people. It would cover her mortgage, and she didn't want to sell her one remaining asset in case this was the biggest mistake of her life.

Today was her last therapy session with Dr. Buckner before departing on her great adventure. Punkin had been in therapy since Alex's suicide, and Dr. Buckner had been a big help. Opal Buckner was a lovely Southern woman, who always smelled of *Toujours moi*, the French perfume that Punkin's Aunt Nina wore. Opal was the kind of woman you would like to have for a mother, older sister, or best friend. She had a "honey-dipped" accent from her home state of Mississippi, and was about Big P's age. She and Punkin got along famously.

During her months of therapy, Punkin had explored her relationship with Alex and her interaction with men in general. Opal helped her discover that she made bad choices in men, putting up boundaries to intimacy. She helped Punkin see that this might have been the result of the claustrophobic love of her doting parents. She felt smothered by them, and it scared her when someone got too close. She was afraid she could not live up to their expectations. All the men she had loved had either been emotionally or legally unavailable. The fact that her fiancé had committed suicide and seemed to have conflicted feelings about his sexuality, brought the point clearly home.

Punkin arrived at Dr. Buckner's office right on time. The Texas heat was abating a bit, this being early September. Dr. Buckner greeted her with a big hug.

"I am happy that you have made a decision about the next step in your life. I hope the journal writing has been helping you see your daily progress and evolution."

Punkin began twisting her pearls.

"I do like writing in my journal. It gets my day started and relieves a little of my anxiety. I think I have made a good decision to move to Paris, but I am scared to death."

Dr. Buckner reassuringly took her hand.

"This is a huge step for you, and I applaud your decision. We have discussed how self-indulged you were as a child and un-realistic about life. And I will repeat, you do have a pattern of falling for unavailable men."

"I surely hope you are not correct. I have always been such a romantic. I wanted that dream of the white picket fence, a happy marriage and lots of children."

Punkin said a little defensively.

"Getting married is one thing, but having children is another. You could have had a child on your own. You have been successful with plenty of money. In today's world, having a child without marriage is no big deal."

"Geez Dr. B, I sometimes feel like a weirdo."

Dr. Buckner laughed and continued.

"You know dear child, I am here to help you look at your life more clearly and objectively."

Punkin was fidgeting in her chair.

"I know, but it is painful!"

"No pain, no gain, as the cliché goes. You have been quite courageous in handling the suicide and sudden passing of your mother."

"I think my mother would be proud of me. I have told you about our wonderful travels together after my father left us. We always ended up in Paris."

Punkin felt a lump rising in her throat.

"What do your girlfriends think about the move?"

That got Punkin's attention and she sat straight up in the chair.

"They think I am NUTS!"

"They may envy you. Have you ever thought of that? You have the freedom to change your life without compromising," Dr. B said

"I guess you are right if you look at it that way. It is sad to me that I have no husband or children, but if I did, I wouldn't be able to do exactly what I wanted to do."

"That is a healthy way to look at it. Turn a negative into a positive. How are you fixed in the money department? I assume Paris is a very expensive city."

"Well, I do have my mother's inheritance and I made a little profit on the sale of my company. I think I have enough money to live in Paris in grand style for at least one year. Then, who knows?"

Punkin was still so unrealistic about money. Paris would be a lot more expensive than Houston.

"Be careful there. You are still young, but at 50 it would be hard to start another career or work for someone else."

"I hear you, but my whole life I have relied on my instincts. I feel something good is going to come out of this."

Dr. Buckner looked at her watch. The session was about to come to an end. In Punkin's opinion, therapists always seemed to stop when one was on a roll. They talked a few more minutes about France, her new apartment and the logistics of such a big trans-Atlantic move.

"You know you can always reach me by e-mail or phone. May I say *bonne chance* and *bon voyage?*"

Punkin looked surprised.

"Dr. B, you speak French!"

"I took it in high school. You are not the only one who loves France."

"You said it just right. Good luck and safe travels for me!"

They finished the session and did plan to stay in touch. After leaving the office, Punkin sat in her car in the parking lot listening to a favorite song of hers and Alex on the oldies station. "*Hearts on Fire, love desire, high and higher….*", sang Earth, Wind and Fire.

Punkin sat transfixed, not able to move. That life was gone. What next?

CHAPTER 5

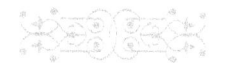

C'est Si Bon

September 15, 2000

"Je suis arrivee, I have arrived. My apartment is just swell. The Eiffel Tower is so close you feel you could touch it. Little Maurice loves it too. SO many doggie friends to meet. I love looking out my window at the Eiffel Tower. It changes from hour to hour with light and weather. Maybe I didn't screw up after all."

Punkin's impressions of Paris matched all her expectations. She loved the pealing of the church bells, the rumble of the underground metro, and the seagulls on the Seine. Late at night laughter would come up to her window from the street 5 floors below. Everyone in Paris always seemed in a good mood. The distinct sound of clicking high heels on the pavement late at night made Punkin wonder where these women had been.

And, there were the exotic smells, which Punkin thought particular to Paris. To her, the city smelled of baking bread and fresh flowers, mixed with perfume, cigarette smoke, and bus fumes. There were yummy aromas, too. One of her neighbors was always preparing *Boeuf Bourguignon*. The smell of the beef, wine, and garlic simmering in a pot wafted through the hallways.

Punkin's little fox terrier, Maurice, had adapted quickly to his new home. He found many "doggie friends" on their walks in the *Bois de Boulogne*. The French took their dogs everywhere. You would see them sitting at the feet of their master in the park or at a *brasserie* or *bistro*. They were as well behaved as their owners.

The light of the city was incredible. Paris was called the City of Light for a reason. The sparkle of the gold leaf on her favorite bridge, *le pont Alexandre*, or on the *Opera Garnier* seemed almost unworldly. Dusk was her favorite time of day. That is when all the lights of Paris came on and illuminated the great monuments and bridges. Everything sparkled. She could understand why this city had been inspiration for painters, writers, photographers, or anyone else with a creative bent.

Her apartment did not disappoint either. It was located in the chic 16th *arrondissement* on *Avenue President Wilson*, across the Seine from the Eiffel Tower. The building was *Haussmannian* in style, built in 1910. It had immense wooden doors, 20 feet high, at the entrance. Upon entering the building, there was an actual carriage way, and old stables at the back of the courtyard. She could just imagine fine ladies and gentlemen of the early 20th century, descending from their carriages to go up the grand carved staircase with its lovely *Aubusson* carpet. The only modernization had taken place in the 1990's when an elevator was installed.

Her apartment was on the 5th floor so it got lots of light. The fabulous view of the Eiffel Tower would change hourly depending on the weather and time of day. Punkin began photographing the Tower from her windows, and was making a collage she hoped to sell. The apartment was very large by French standards. In its almost 1500 square feet were two spacious bedrooms, 2 bathrooms, a large kitchen, dining room and living room. She planted bright red geraniums on the terrace that gave every room an unobstructed view of the Tower. The owner had put a marble table and two wrought iron chairs on the terrace leading from the living room.

The apartment was furnished in elegant "hand-me-downs" from the owners' mother who had lived in the apartment. Old *Napoleon III commodes*, a massive Art Deco dining room table and chairs, and cushy sofas. Her bedroom had a huge wrought iron bed, and an adjacent bathroom. All this luxury came at a price. Punkin had told the girls at lunch that she has exceeded her budget. The apartment was costing her over $4500 us dollars per month. She would think about that at some other time.

Punkin found getting around Paris was pretty easy. The city had excellent public transportation and she loved riding the bus. In Houston, everyone had a car and no one but the "help" rode a bus. She didn't miss having a car at all.

She now felt like a real Parisian and always rode *le bus*. *Le metro* was excellent, too, but Punkin was a bit of a *claustrophobe*. She did not like being underground, or in enclosed places. The buses made a great whooshing sound when they stopped and rocked from side to side like a big ocean liner. The drivers covered all the bases when greeting passengers. Always saying *bonjour, bonsoir et bon voyage*.

There was every cross-section of humanity on the bus: imperious fashion ladies from the 7th and 16th *arrondissements*; little nuns with God's face; crying babies in strollers, and smelly workmen in overalls. Sometimes, masses of school children, going on a field trip, loaded into the bus. She like to observe what *"tout le monde"* was reading. It was usually *Balzac, Zola* or *Hugo*. There were no *People Magazine* readers in this bunch! Punkin mused that the great *Balzac* could have just rolled out of his bed in the morning and picked up a pen to write the *Comedie Humaine*. There were so many interesting people and situations in Paris, always.

But with life, nothing is perfect, and from time to time the buses could be problematic. There are so many cobblestone streets left in Paris that if a bus hit a pothole, teeth would rattle. At rush hour the buses were packed and Punkin would have to extricate herself with a shoe horn to get off. Demonstrations and strikes were a problem, too. The French love to protest, and these *manifestations* and *greves* could bring the whole city to a halt. Drivers would stop without explanation and everyone would have to get out of the bus.

This crisp autumn day in September, Punkin was on the bus going to the American Club. This organization, quite prestigious, was the oldest ex-pat club in Paris, founded by Benjamin Franklin.

It had started to rain a bit, and she watched from the bus window as umbrellas unfurled and *les gens de Paris* hustled to find shelter.

Sitting next to her on the bus was an impeccably dressed woman who she assumed was French. Punkin began to engage her in conversation.

"*Bonjour*"

Punkin turned on her most enticing grin.

The French woman returned Punkin's smile and said.

"*Bonjour, Vous parlez francais ?*"

"*Un peu*, but I am American. *Est-ce que vous parlez anglais ?*"

(If a French person thinks you speak French, they break into English. It is kind of a competition thing.)

"*Ooof*, always so many Americans in Paris. Are you staying long?"

"The rest of my life, I hope".

Punkin got a thrill out of saying this, and continued.

"Do you mind if we chat a bit?"

"*Pas de tout*, certainly, I do not *descende* for three more stops."

"In the rain I always have such trouble balancing everything: my umbrella; purse; shopping bags. I have fallen several times trying to keep my balance on the wet streets."

It was true. Punkin had never taken a fall in the U.S., but since arriving in Paris, she had tumbled a couple of times, skinning her knees, but always bounced back up.

"You learn to manage. My rule is to never pick up anything during the day that you can't carry home at night. And since it rains so much in Paris in the fall and winter, I always carry a *chapeau* instead of an umbrella."

"HOW do French women manage on those heels?"

"Ah, yes, those *talons* are for the very young."

Punkin began to gush.

"I love how elegant everyone looks with a beautiful scarf, handbag and shoes."

The French woman was warming up to Punkin. If one loves France, the French are always ready to talk to you.

"*Oui, les francaises* are *toujours chic*. You Americans seem to wear white tennis shoes, and athletic apparel even when not exercising."

Punkin laughed.

"Yes we can be a little sloppy when traveling, but not me."

"How you find Paris?"

"It is absolute magic. I have to pinch myself sometimes. I feel like I am living in a *Renoir* painting or on a movie set."

"That is very *poetique*. Those with an artistic spirit get along well here."

With that remark, the woman pushed the big red button at the bus doors to signal she wanted to get off at the next stop. She turned to Punkin and said,

"*Au revoir*. I hope you enjoy your stay in Paris."

The big bus doors opened and she was gone.

A few more stopes and Punkin was in the *premier arrondissement*, 1st district, and the location of the American Club. It was housed in an 18th century building on the *Place de la Concorde* which at one time had been called *Place de Louis XIV* before the French Revolution. The Club was situated close to the 5-star *Hotel Crillon*. Punkin entered the building's lavish reception hall decorated in the style of *Louis XVI*, and felt a little intimidated. She was at heart a little shy, although one would never guess it. Almost immediately, she noticed a beautiful blonde in a magnificent sable coat and cowboy hat heading in her direction.

"Excuse me. I am looking for someone with the American Club".

"Hi. Maybe I can help. I am a new member. Name is Suzie Gilmore."

She stuck out her hand and shook Punkin's.

Punkin detected her Southern accent.

"Hi. My name is Punkin Lowery. You sound Southern like me."

"Right you are darlin'. I am from Georgia. You have quite the Southern accent yourself."

"You got me. You can take the girl out of Texas but not Texas out of the girl. I am from Houston."

"Been in Paris long?"

"All of three weeks. I just moved here. What about you?"

"I have been here about three months. I left a bum husband, picked up my two kids and headed across the pond."

There was a story here and Punkin wanted to get to know this girl better. She liked her spirit.

"Sorry to hear about your husband. I moved here by myself. Maybe that makes it easier."

"We have done OK. I found a great furnished apartment on *rue st. peres* in the 6th, off of *blvd. St Germain*. My kids love living here, and I do, too. Don't you find Paris fabulous? It is so different from the US."

"I absolutely love it. But I agree, it is different. There is nothing open 24/7 like there is in the US."

"I know what you mean. You are shit out of luck if you need to buy a bottle of milk at 11pm on a weekend. Where are those U-Totems when you need 'em?"

Suzie let out an infectious laugh. Punkin was liking this girl. Maybe they could become running buddies.

"I guess you are thinking about joining the Club? We have both American and French members. In fact, you picked a good day to visit. I am meeting the President of the Club and his wife for a luncheon here today. I am sure they wouldn't mind you joining us."

"Thanks. That is so kind. I don't know many people in Paris yet."

The girls checked their coats at the *vestiare*, and went in the direction of the ballroom where many tables were set up for lunch. There was a bar at the end of the room where they were serving *aperitifs*. A tall man with a distinguished looking eye-patch strolled by and gave them the greeting of *bonjour*.

Suzie turned to Punkin and whispered in her ear.

"That is Jean Aumont. His grandfather was with *de Gaulle* at the liberation of Paris. He is retired military, just back from Algeria. His family owns a vineyard in Bordeaux, and they are rollin' in the dough."

"Is he married?"

(The first question any single girl asks)

"I think he is divorced. I find him a little *triste* with only one good eye. Wonder how he lost the other one?"

"I think that eye-patch makes him look interesting. It might be fun to get to know him better."

Punkin was always on the hunt for a man.

"Watch out there. I hear his mother is a holy terror. You know French mothers never think American girls are good enough for their sons."

"Thanks for the tip. Have you met anyone yet?"

"No, I am purposely taking it slow. I've got to divorce the bastard husband first. What about you?"

"Yes, I have. My landlord is dreamy and a real French Count! He is 40, but married."

"Well you can't have everything. From what I can tell, married or single, French men like older women and American women. I think they believe we are more 'free' in the sex department."

Suzie was getting a little naughty and Punkin loved it.

"I agree. It is not all about youth, big boobs and too-white teeth like in the US. A woman my age is thought to be over the hill in America."

"If it is any consolation, you do not look 'middle aged'. I just turned 40 myself."

Suzie and Punkin lingered at the bar with their *kirs*, an *aperitif* with white wine and *cassis*. An older couple approached and greeted Suzie. This must be the President of the Club and his wife, Punkin surmised.

The man looked about 65 with sparkling brown eyes and a charming smile. He was carrying a man purse, which Punkin thought so continental. You wouldn't see any big brawny Texas men carrying a purse! He was also perfectly attired in a double-breasted suit and what looked like an *Hermes* tie. His wife was equally elegant in head to toe *Chanel*. Punkin guessed she was near the same age as her husband, but looked much younger with great effect.

Suzie greeted them with *bisous*, kisses on both cheeks, and started the introductions.

"Punkin, I would like you to meet Tom and Eleanor Charleson."

Eleanor extended her hand that was covered in diamonds.

"*Bonjour et Bienvenue..*"

"*Enchante*, it is so nice to meet you. I just met Suzie and was telling her I would love to join the Club."

"I didn't think I had seen you here before. I always notice pretty girls," said Tom

"We are always looking for new members. We have a membership of 50% American and 50% French and other nationalities," Tom continued.

"But of course, you have to be nominated by two members to be considered", Eleanor chimed in with a haughty tone.

"I am sure we can find sponsors for Punkin," said Tom, giving his wife an icy stare.

"That would be swell! I have only been here a couple of weeks and do not know many people. How long have you all been here?"

"We have been in Paris for 30 years and are originally from Georgia like Suzie. After I retired from my brokerage firm we decided to stay," said Tom as he winked at Punkin.

"We just adore it here. You must meet our little dash hound, Clementine. She goes everywhere with us," Eleanor added.

Punkin was thrilled to meet "dog people" and people from the South.

"Oh how wonderful. I have a dog, too. Clementine must meet my terrier Maurice."

A waiter approached the bar with a tiny bell which he rang to announce lunch was served.

"There's the starting bell," laughed Tom

He guided the girls and Eleanor through the crowd which now numbered around 100 to get a good table close to the speaker's table. Today's speaker was a member of the *Assemble Nationale*, France's Senate. His talk was expected to be interesting, considering world events. France was having its problems, too.

An average Parisian lunch can take three hours. This American Club *dejeuner* was no exception. During the 4-course meal with wines, the conversation flowed. The foursome found they had a lot in common besides their Southern heritage. They all loved to play bridge and made plans to get together at the Charleson's apartment the following week for a couple of rubbers.

PARIS PERFECT

Punkin learned a lot about living in Paris during the lunch. She would have to spend more money than she thought to keep up with this crowd. France was still on the *franc* monetary system so she did make money when she changed dollars. She would worry about running out of money later.

CHAPTER 6

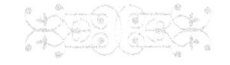

I'll Take Romance

Paris, September 30, 2000

"*So many interesting characters to observe here. The old chrone who is always on the Avenue Foch. She is obviously homeless and continually wandering the 16ᵗ in her dark rags and shoes covered in cloth. She carries a cane with a point on the end and is constantly chasing the pigeons in the park. I guess that point is to skewer them for dinner, but they are too fast for her. Where does she go, I wonder, when it gets dark, and the city is cold and rainy? There are so many homeless people here. They are mostly men just wanting a handout to buy another cheap bottle of wine. But I hate seeing the small children that sit on my street all day long, on a suitcase with a beggar's cup, and no food it appears. I asked my local policeman, why these children were not in school. He sadly said the police had no way to register them if their parents were illegals. How sad...*"

What Punkin had told Suzie about her landlord was true. He was a Count, and very easy on the eyes. His full name was *Sebastian, le comte de Richmond*. He was from an old French family whose ancestors had worked for a king or two. His wife's family, the Castellanes, were *nouveau*, making their money in the publishing business. What counted in *la belle france* was your family tree. It had better go back a couple of centuries. Sebastian's family did and he had the title. He and his wife Michelle had grown up together. As Punkin got to know Sebastian better she discovered the two were more friends than lovers. Perhaps Michelle had married him for his title. That was done all the time in France.

Sebastian was a documentary filmmaker, and worked for *Canal Arte*, similar to the American Channel, *PBS*. With all Michelle's money, he could indulge his creative bent. Like most French men, he was short, around 5 feet 8 inches tall. Punkin towered over him. He had dark brown hair, penetrating and sensitive brown eyes, and a wonderful sense of humor. There was a sexual heat radiating from him. She wondered what it would be like to go to bed with him.

As she got settled into her apartment, he was always coming around with one excuse or another. He was a real handyman and could fix anything. Since Punkin's apartment was very old, there were always things to be repaired. They joked that he was *Monsieur Bricolage*, a character on French TV. Since Sebastian's in-laws lived right next door, no one thought anything of his frequent visits. The Castellanes had put him in charge of renting the apartment and inter-acting with the *locataire*, renter.

As their friendship deepened, there was an unspoken feeling that they both wanted to take the relationship to a more *intime* level. Punkin knew there was no future in it, but she needed to feel close to a man again.

One cold fall day, when the leaves on the chestnut trees were turning a brilliant orange/gold, she was lying in bed looking at the Eiffel Tower. She loved the fall with colder weather. All her life she felt energized when the summer was over and autumn arrived. She felt this time of year brought new beginnings. She was sipping *café*, and writing her morning e-mails to her friends in the US. She knew they would not be up for hours, but it made her feel closer to them, kind of like talking on the telephone.

Little Maurice was stretched out at the foot of her big wrought iron bed, a turn-of-the-century number that had been the grandmother's. Hanging over the bed was a portrait in pastels of a man and a woman in an intimate embrace. Punkin had been struck by this *tableau* when she first moved in. It looked remarkably like her and Sebastian.

Punkin heard the doorbell ring. She wondered who it could be at this early hour. Her *gardienne*, Catherine, never let anyone in the building she did not know. Punkin quickly put on her *peignoir* and went to the door. Standing there with a fresh French *baguette* was Sebastian. How cute he looked in his red muffler and brown suede shoes. French men always wore suede shoes, no matter the season. How young he looked.

"*Bonjour*, Punkin"

He pronounced her name like "pookin" which she found adorable.

"*Desole si je vous derange*, didn't mean to disturb, but I was next door at the in-laws and thought I would bring you a little *petit-dejeuner*".

Punkin was pleased to see him. She had nothing in the house for breakfast. A thought crossed her mind that she had no make-up on. She must look a fright. She kissed him on both cheeks, and invited him in. They went down the long hallway to the kitchen with Maurice following. His little toenails made a tapping sound on the wood floor like a snare drum.

As Sebastian sliced the bread, she got the jam out of the *frigo*, refrigerator, and made more coffee. They sat down at the little table to eat, their elbows lightly touching.

"Would you like to join me today at *Le Louvre*? I am filming a segment on Louis XVI and Marie Antoinette. It will accompany a new exposition at the museum."

Punkin's heart skipped a bit. Maybe today their relationship would deepen.

"It is such a beautiful day, I thought you might like to ride there on my motorcycle", he continued.

"I would love to! But if you don't want me to go like this, you had better leave for a while and then come back. What time should I be ready?"

"I will be back in 1 hour and then *zoot zoot*, on to the Louvre."

Sebastian smiled deeply into her eyes. She felt that look down to her toes.

They finished their breakfast in quiet conversation, their arms always touching. She walked Sebastian to the door and then started talking to Maurice. He was her sounding board on all things important.

"Oh *mon petit chien*, we have to walk you and then I must look *tres chic* for my date. You will need to stay in the kitchen until I get back."

She reached down and scratched his ears. She swore he could always understand every word she said.

Punkin dressed in a hurry, no time to wash her hair, so she wrapped an *Hermes* scarf around her hair and put on big gold hoop earrings. Those and her designer sun-glasses would make her look quite chic.

The grandiose 18th century Grandfather clock in the entry way chimed the hour and the half-hour. It had taken some getting used to. She heard it strike 10, and almost immediately there was Sebastian's knock at the door. He had a helmet for her that he lovingly placed on her head, and they were off.

Sebastian was a maniac driver, she discovered. They were going at break-neck speed along the *quai* that leads from the 16th to the *Pont Alma,* past the *Pont Neuf,* and on to the Louvre. She held on for dear life. It was comforting and a little stimulating to hold on to Sebastian's waist. She could feel his ribcage expand and contract as he breathed. She thought he smelled divine.

They got to the Louvre in record time. She noticed that Sebastian's crew were already assembled as were the two actors portraying Louis and Marie. They were dressed in the magnificent fashion of the court of Louis XVI.

The Louvre was a dazzling site with its 17th century architecture and the lush *Tuileries* gardens. She thought, however, that the glass pyramid, designed by IM Pei, as the new entrance, looked out of place. There had been much discussion and competition among the world's finest architects to get the commission, but she didn't like it.

Sebastian settled Punkin on a bench leading into the gardens with a view of the "Mini Arc", a small replica of the *Arc de Triomphe*. At the top of the mini was a statue of Napoleon in a chariot driving a team of 6 horses. It was all done in gold leaf. It gleamed like a gigantic ring in the bright sunshine.

"*Cherie*, I will leave you now and when we break for lunch, we can have a little picnic under the trees. I hope you will not be bored. Filming can be so slow."

Sebastian gave her a peck on the cheek and returned to the center courtyard of the Louvre. Punkin observed Sebastian as he went through his paces as a director. She noticed he had a gentle way with all and from time to time, he cast a meaningful glance her way.

Punkin had plenty of time to survey her surroundings. She watched all variety of people in the gardens, sitting in the green metal chairs, or gathering around the large fountain in the middle of the gardens. The chestnut trees made a soft whistling sound as they swayed in the breeze.

She began to think about her past life and what the future might hold. At that moment, she knew that she had made the right decision to move to Paris.

About 1pm, the film crew broke for lunch and Sebastian returned with a little picnic basket filled with sandwiches and of course, a bottle of red wine. The French, *jamais*, never, eat a meal without wine. He sat close to her as they began to talk about film.

"You may not know this about me, but I am very interested in French films, especially the old ones made by Jean Renoir and the *nouvelle vague* guys, Truffaut, Goddard and Maule. I even love Jean-Pierre Melville," said Punkin sliding just a little bit closer to him.

"You know of Jean-Pierre Melville? Most Americans have never heard of him."

"Yes, I love *film noir*, and all those *Cahiers du Cinema* guys. You of course know they were all film journalists before they started the *nouvelle vague* screen movement. In my opinion, they revolutionized French film."

Sebastian was impressed.

"I always wanted that cute short haircut that Jean Seberg wore in *Breathless*, "she added.

Sebastian had taken off her scarf and was stroking her long hair.

"My *petite chou*, do not ever cut your hair. I love it long. You are looking more Parisian every day."

He moved closer to her on the bench, and began tracing her face with his hand.

"Do you also know much about French history?'

"*Bien sur*, of course. I am a history buff, too. I have read so much about the time of Franklin, Jefferson and Adams in Paris and those grand literary salons of people like *Madame de Sevigny*. I also admire early French women authors like George Sand. Maybe I lived in the 18th century in a past life."

"So I guess you know about Louis and Marie?"

"From what I have read, I do not think they are as evil as they were portrayed in all those movies. I believe, sadly, they were just naïve and out of touch with their people. I remember reading that if they had stayed in Paris, connected to the people, and not left for *Versailles*, there may not have been a Revolution."

"A very wise observation, Punkin."

They finished their lunch and Sebastian went back to finish the day's shooting. Before leaving her he gave her a real kiss on the lips, with a little tongue involved. She started to tingle. She wanted to grab him, and make love right there. *Calme toi*, she said to herself.

She took a short walk into the *Tuileries* and up to the fountain near the *Musee L' Orangerie*. The Paris sky was the color of pale blue satin with tufts of puffy white clouds. She sat for a moment in one of the chairs and listened to the wind. She was truly content.

The filming continued just until sunset. She walked back to the Louvre where Sebastian was waiting.

"I wouldn't mind *quelque chose a boire*. I would love a good glass of wine, how about you?" Sebastien said as he gave her another kiss.

"That sounds grand. Where do you suggest we go?"

Punkin was trying to retain her composure, but every nerve in her body was pulsating.

"I love jazz and I know this great little wine bar near *Notre Dame*. It is called the Black Cat, *Le Chat Noir*.

"Sounds intriguing. *On y va*. Let's go!"

They got back on the cycle and zipped down the *quai* again just a short distance to the bar. The sun was setting over the monuments. The city has a wonderful amber glow. They arrived at the Black Cat, famous since the days of Hemingway and Fitzgerald.

As Sebastian helped Punkin down from the bike, he took off her helmet, cupped her face in his hands and gave her a long lingering French kiss. She was right. She had thought he would be a great kisser and he was. Her philosophy was that if a man was a great kisser he would also be very good in bed. This might be the night.

The club was perfect for lovers. As one would imagine in a novel, it was dark, smoky, and pulsating with music and sex. They sat down at a *banquette* near the dance floor, sitting very close. The jazz combo has just begun a Miles Davis riff.

"What would you like besides me?" Sebastian grinned like a Cheshire Cat.

"Wow, pardner, let's start with something to drink first."

"How about a bottle of Burgundy? Then you can tell me your life story."

"Good choice. I love the wines of Burgundy, much better than Bordeaux. They were now sitting so close together, that their lips almost touched when they talked. The wine arrived and Punkin began to talk about herself.

"About me, I had a business of my own, advertising, which I poured all my energies into. And then my fiancé, who I loved more than life, committed suicide. Then my mother died. Those nightmares are why I have escaped here."

It was all pouring out of Punkin. She wanted to tell this man everything.

"*Ma pauvre*, I had no idea. You always seem so cheerful."

"Thanks, but all those things really threw me for a loop."

Sebastian looked perplexed.

"What is this 'loop' thing?"

She laughed.

"Oh, I forgot. That is American slang. I know we made a deal that I would teach you our slang if you would teach me the French.

Throwing for a loop means something puts you off-center. Normally it is a situation you can't control."

"I understand. I have never lost anyone close to me except my father and that was tough. My poor *maman* is still not over it, and he has been gone for 10 years."

"I have loved France since I was 16 and I have not been disappointed. I love everything about this country. The language sounds like music, and the beauty of the city just takes my breath away. The only word to describe it is magic."

Punkin began to feel the effects of the wine. This time it was she who cupped Sebastian's face in her hands and gave him a monster, wet kiss which just kept on going. The great thing is no one paid any attention. Public displays of affection were common in Paris, the City of Lovers.

She took a deep breath. It was now or never.

"We Americans are quite direct. I find you so attractive and when we first met I felt a little '*frisson*'."

Le Chat was out of the bag.

"*Merci*, and truthfully I might say I felt the same thing, like we had known each other before. My marriage after 15 years is not too satisfying. Michelle and I are more like roommates than lovers. Let's get out of here and go to your place. My family is in the country and I can stay all night."

The two did not talk much on the ride home. Punkin was getting quite aroused and wet, and she was sure if she could feel Sebastian's crotch, it would be growing. He would barely let her unlock the door before he was undressing her. She had purposely worn sexy lace underwear hoping that this might happen. The barking of Maurice in the kitchen cooled the flames of passion for a moment.

"*Zoot*, I must take Maurice out for a short walk. He has been cooped up in the kitchen all day. Make yourself comfortable and I will be right back."

Punkin ran out the door with Maurice on his leash and they were back in record time. Poor Maurice, he needed longer to do his doggie business, but he wasn't getting it tonight. She put Maurice back into the warm kitchen and came into the living room. Sebastian had lit a fire and had completely undressed. He was lying on the sofa with the fur throw wrapped around him.

"*Viens, Cherie.* I want to see you naked."

Punkin began disrobing in the most alluring fashion. She was totally uninhibited about undressing in front of Sebastian, when normally she would be quite shy. Now in just her panties, she threw back the throw to expose Sebastian's body. He had a mighty erection. She melted into his arms.

"I want to have the sex with you."

It was so cute the way he said it.

"Don't you want something to eat or drink first?"

"Maybe a little of the wine we brought back. I want to drink it out of your belly button."

Reaching for the bottle of Burgundy, he took a big drink and then poured some wine into her belly button and started lapping it up. Punkin gave out the most lascivious laugh. She was delighted and surprised. How liberating these French men can be! She was so loud, she hoped her stuffy neighbors hadn't heard. She was supposed to be living alone.

Sebastian began to explore her body. He took off her panties and began caressing her long legs, kissing her down to her toes. When he saw her toenails were painted a bright red, he squealed.

"I love your toes!"

Punkin knew what was next.

"Do you have any *preservatifs?*"

This question was a new one for her. She thought it sounded like he wanted some jam. Then realized he was talking about condoms. Duh!

"Oh.. you mean rubbers. I wasn't expecting this, so let me go see."

She got up to go into the master bathroom. The light from the fire illuminated her naked body, all 6 feet of it. She felt the warmth of the fire on her bare skin. Luckily she found some condoms in her make up bag.

When she came back to the sofa, he had turned on some soft, classical music. He was a tender as well as athletic lover.

"Ohhh, that hurts a bit. Guess it has been too long for me," she said as he entered her.

Sebastian slowed his motion and hugged her tighter to him.

"Relax *Cherie*. I will go slow."

Their lovemaking continued at a tender pace. When it was over, Punkin felt drained of all bodily fluids.

"I need some water. My mouth is so dry. Do you want anything?"

"Just you, *mon amour*. Don't be long."

He reluctantly let her get up and he snuggled deeper back into the fur cover.

Punkin returned quickly after drinking about a liter of water. She checked on Maurice who had become a little excited with all the lovemaking noises. She patted him and gave him a doggie treat before returning to the living room.

Coming back to the sofa, Sebastian entwined her in his arms. At that moment, there was nobody else in the world but them.

"I have been meaning to ask you. Do you think that painting over my bed looks like you and me? I think of that every morning when I get up."

(One of the great things about having sex is that when it's over, you can talk to your partner about anything.)

"Now that you mention it, that painting does look like us. It has always been over the bed. Michelle and I lived here briefly after we married and it was there then. I have no idea who painted it. Maybe it means our meeting was a *fait accompli*, just meant to be."

"Have you had many affairs?"

Punkin was not afraid to hear the answer.

"Yes, a few. French men love beautiful women and their wives expect them to have a little *affaire* from time to time. I do not take one lightly. I have to feel something special about the woman, as I do for you."

He said the perfect thing.

"Maybe next time I should dress in a garter belt and lace stockings, if I am going to be your mistress," she giggled.

"*Tres bien, bravo!* I would love for you to dress up for me."

The time flew by, and when the big clock in the hallway chimed 3am, neither of them had any idea what time it was.

"*Mon dieu*, I guess I should be getting home. I do not want Catherine to see me. She knows my family is in the country. She is a great *gardienne*, but so nosey, like most of them."

He reluctantly began putting on his clothes that were piled around the sofa.

"Oh *merde*, I remember I have a date to play bridge this morning at 10 at my new friends, the Charlesons.

Sebastian dressed, and Punkin went to her bedroom to put on a terrycloth robe. She walked him to the door, hearing Maurice bark once again in the kitchen. She probably would have to take him downstairs before she went to bed.

At the door, Sebastian impulsively grabbed her, opened her robe, and pressed her naked body next to his. He held her for an instant in a strong embrace, giving her one last long kiss.

"*Bonne nuit*, good night, *cherie*".

He said, in the softest voice, before he closed the door.

Punkin was back in the saddle of love, again.

CHAPTER 7

A Grand Slam and a Cause

Punkin got to sleep around 4. She dreamed of Sebastian. Her alarm clock went off at 9, followed by the booming of the hall clock. She dressed in her sweats to take Maurice out for his morning walk. There was a lot of wind this fall day, and a little frost in the air. She thought she had better take a hat on her excursion to the Charlesons. She had a cute little French *chapeau* with felt ribbons of red, yellow and green. It would look *tres chic* with her long red wool coat and plaid muffler.

She feed Maurice, and got dressed more warmly. She might have to stand at the bus stop for a long time. It was always a little uncomfortable standing there in inclement weather. Today she was in luck. The 63 bus arrived in 10 minutes and it was a straight shot down *Blvd. St Germain* to the Charleson's apartment in the 7th arrondissement on *St. Germain* at *rue de bac*. This was prime Paris real estate.

She arrived right at 10am and entered their building. An impressive early 20th century like hers with the same immense wooden doors at the entrance. *Haussmannian* architecture was the same for all these buildings. They had tile inlay floors at the entrance, grand staircases, and *Aubusson* red rugs as runners up the stairs. She pressed the numbers for their outside door code and took the elevator to the 3rd floor. When she exited the elevator, she was surprised to see Suzie standing there. She had not seen her at the *entrée*.

"Heh Suze, good timing. Where did you come from?"

She kissed Suzie on both cheeks.

"I took the stairs. I need some exercise after all the good food and wine I have been imbibing," she said, a little out of breath.

They rang the Charleson's bell and Tom came to the door.

"*Bonjour jeunes filles*, come in. Eleanor is in the living room. We are looking forward to some fast and furious bridge today."

The Charleson's living room was chock-a-block with Persian rugs, Ming vases, *Louis XV* furniture and all kinds of other *bibelots* (or as one would say in English, brick a brack). The rugs were piled on top of each other, so it was difficult to walk. The *salon* looked like something out of Dicken's *Curiosity Shop*. Eleanor could see the girl's reactions to all the clutter.

"Hi girls, I guess you think we are pack rats. Tom and I can never resist buying on our trips abroad, and the *marche aux puces*, flea market has great bargains."

"I think everything looks so French," said Punkin

"I do know about the great bargains at the *puce,* especially if you bring cash," added Suzie

"Yes, the American buyers just are not coming any longer and the antique dealers are really suffering out there," said Eleanor.

It was only a little after 10 in the morning but Tom asked,

"Anyone want a bloody mary? I am going to have one to whet my whistle."

"I think I'll pass but I would love some *café,* "said Punkin still trying to wake up from her late night.

"I will join you in that Bloody Mary," said Suzie.

As Tom and Suzie headed into the kitchen, Eleanor and Punkin went into the den where the card table was set. The Charleson's kitchen was large by French standards. It had a big butcher block dining table in the center which accommodated eight, a huge *Aga* stove, and burnished brick walls. *CNN* was playing on the small TV on the kitchen counter. Tom had to keep up with the news in the US, especially news about the financial markets.

"I'll put on a little mood music," he said, as he mixed the bloodies.

"Do you know the musician Chet Baker? He was a great jazz man, American living in Paris in the 60's. Unfortunately, he died too young."

"No, never heard of him. So many musicians die too young of some kind of excess. Sounds like what happened to Jim Morrison," said Suzie taking her spicy Bloody Mary into the den.

'It is a very similar story. Since you mentioned Jim Morrison, have you been to his grave at *Pere Lachaise?* It is a trip. You see old hippies, vagabonds, and the homeless hanging around, usually smoking weed or drinking Jim's favorite Jack Daniels."

Suzie made a peace sign and they both laughed.

In the den, the Charleson's little dash hound, Clementine, was laying under the card table. Maybe Punkin should have brought Maurice. She would ask for the next time.

Eleanor has decided that she and Punkin would be partners for the first rubber. She started to deal and turned to Suzie.

"How are your children adapting to Paris? It is not secret you are coming off a messy divorce. The ex-pat tom toms beat here just like in any small town."

"Thanks for asking. My son, Christopher, seems to like it better than my daughter Charlotte. He is really mastering the French language. You know we are neighbors."

"We are right around the corner on *rue st peres*. I found the most marvelous furnished apartment all outfitted in antiques from the *Louis Philippe* period," she continued as she surveyed her hand.

"In my opinion, the 7th is the best arrondissement," said Eleanor with a rather haughty air.

Punkin was beginning to think she was a real snob.

"I like the 7th but my apartment in the 16th has the most fabulous view of the Eiffel Tower, and is huge. Maybe I can host the group some time."

Punkin was defending her turf.

"Don't leave me out. I would love to have you all over for bridge or drinks, too," said Suzie

"I had an idea. My apartment is so great for entertaining. What are y'all doing for Thanksgiving? Punkin asked.

"We usually do something at home. The French really do not understand this holiday with the Pilgrims and the Indians. Plus, they think *le dinde*, turkey, is a lowly bird," said Tom

"Oh, please come to my house this year. I love to cook, and it will be my first holiday away from the US. I hear there is a restaurant in *Le Marais*, owned by an American and her French chef husband that sells turkey and all the trimmings. I will make it a big party and invite my French neighbors, and my *gardienne*."

Eleanor made a bid and looked up from her cards directly at Punkin.

"Dear Punkin, you never, *jamais*, invite your help to sit at table."

Good God, Punkin thought. Was this chick for real? What an asinine thing to say. She wasn't sure that she and Eleanor would remain friends.

"I love my *gardienne*, and so do all my neighbors. She has been such a big help in getting me settled, and everyone treats Catherine and her husband like family," retorted Punkin.

The foursome really got into the game. By the time they finished their first rubber, it was 12 noon. Eleanor and Punkin had been the big winners. They made a grand slam on the last hand. Punkin was relieved she could hold her own with this group, after not playing bridge much since college.

It was time for a little lunch.

"Let's take a *dejeuner* break. Eleanor has made a wonderful *salade nicoise*, and I can crack open a bottle of *cremant*. Hope you all can stay for a few more games after lunch."

"*Avec plaisir*, I do not need to pick up the kids at the American School until 5pm."

"I am happy to stay as well. I just need to get home at a reasonable time to take Maurice out for this afternoon constitutional."

The group adjoined to the kitchen where they had a delightful lunch with much sparkling wine. It put all in a jolly mood. Around 2pm, they took their coffee and *petits fours* back into the den. It was Punkin's deal and as she passed out the cards, she asked,

"Tom, at the American Club lunch, you mentioned something about the Club's protégé program for young woman down on their luck. I would love to hear more about it."

"It is the most humanitarian endeavor. I have to give Eleanor the credit for thinking it up. We have a group of girls really at the poverty line. Some of their stories would make you cry."

Eleanor bid 3 no trump, and jumped right in.

"We want to give them hope that there is a better life out there. Tom and I are sponsoring a pretty young thing named Madeleine Junot. Hers is the saddest story of all. Her mother died when she was 5 and her father is unknown. She was shuttled around to family members until she was 18, and now is fending for herself."

"How horrible that sounds. It would make a good plot for a Hugo novel."

Punkin said, as she bid 4 spades to her partner Tom. She was intrigued and wanted to know more about Madeleine Junot.

"Want to hear a little gossip?"

Eleanor had a sadistic gleam in her eye.

"Eleanor, shush. There is no need to go into that," said Tom

She gave her husband an icy look and continued.

"As I was saying about Madeleine…she is quite lovely and a talented artist, but a real handful. She has been working the streets of *St. Denis* as a prostitute. You know *St. Denis* is one of the roughest *banlieues* outside Paris. I am told she has a pimp who will not let her go. He has some strange hold over her."

Our Texas girl looked shocked.

"A pimp? Lordy, Lordy."

"Yes my dear, and he has been threatening the Club."

"Eleanor, that is enough. You have been watching too many movies. I am sure he is harmless and nothing will come of it," said Tom reassuringly.

"That girl sounds like t-r-o-u-b-l-e to me", said Suzie.

"Oh Suzie, have a heart. Sometimes one is just dealt a bad hand in life," said Punkin

"I am sorry but I agree with Eleanor. This pimp of Madeleine's could be dangerous."

"We have a meeting with the protégés at the American Cathedral in two weeks. The churches in Paris have been our referral source for these girls," said Tom, trying to get off the pimp issue.

"I would love to come Tom," said Punkin.

Paris was grand, but she needed a cause. She was feeling kind of restless and adrift.

"Wonderful! What about you, Suzie?"

"Count me in. With the children at school all day, I don't have much to do."

"Maybe one of you can connect with Madeleine, being closer to her age. I think Tom and I are a little too old for her," Eleanor said.

Punkin was amazed Eleanor would admit that she was older.

The game finished around 4pm. Tom and Suzie won this round, and it had been a good way to spend the day. Before the girls left, Eleanor gave them the address of the Cathedral and start time for the meeting.

CHAPTER 8

Paris, October 20, 2000

"Life continues to be divine here. Sebastian has turned out to be a blessing. He is a wonderful lover, and I don't even mind being a 'kept woman', ha-ha! Getting a lot colder. I love it. The trees are gold and orange, there is a nip in the air so invigorating, and I finally am not scared to death to open the front door and go out into the world. I told myself 'baby steps', one day at a time, and it is getting easier. I have to remind myself I do speak the language, and rather well, if I do say so myself. I get compliments all the time. Today is a new adventure. Going to the American Club meeting on their protégé program. It will give me something worthwhile to do rather than just be a one of those Americans in Paris who just eats, drinks and talks a good game."

Madeleine Junot

She was the raw material of a divinity-Thomas Hardy

Life had not been a bed of roses for Punkin in Paris. She got terribly lonely at times. She had "things" to occupy her days, but she did not want to become one of those *ex-pats* one saw around Paris. *Poseurs* who talked a good game, and seemed to live a lavish lifestyle, but it was all 'smoke and mirrors'. Although she loved being with Sebastian, his visits were short. "Hello, let's make love, and good-bye." That was the saga with a married man. She was falling back into her old pattern of unavailable men. She was enjoying him and didn't want to think about regressing.

When the walls closed in, she would take a walk in the *Bois de Boulogne*, and end up at some sidewalk café near *La Muette*. She would sip her café and watch the world go by. She thought about poor Madeleine Junot. She was a young woman with a hard life, something Punkin knew nothing about in her sheltered life. She might be able to help.

The next two weeks passed quickly. Punkin's friend Janey came for a visit from Texas. It was a bit stressful because Janey could do nothing by herself. She did not speak the language, and expected Punkin to be a constant tour guide. She discovered that she didn't have much in common with Janey any longer. They promised to stay in touch, but in her heart she hoped none of the other Birthday Club girls would visit. Paris was changing her.

Winter was settling in. It rarely snowed in Paris, but today in late October, there were some flurries. It made the city look like something in a snow globe. The meeting of the protégé program was today at the American Cathedral.

Punkin decided not to wear her mink coat, although the weather warranted it. She thought it too "grand'. She put on her standby long red coat and added a cute red brim wool hat. She looked kind of like a Cardinal at the Vatican, but cute!

The American Cathedral on *Avenue George V* was just a 10-minute walk away. The Cathedral is a magnificent edifice built in 1889 for wealthy ex-pat Americans like J.P. Morgan. It was designed by English architect Edmond Street. The odd thing is, it does not have a bell tower. All great Cathedrals have a bell tower.

The Cathedral was quite renowned in Paris. A painting of it by artist, *Jean Berard* depicting the Cathedral on Christmas morning 1890, hung in the city's history museum. *Le Carnavalet*. Many excellent Deans had shepherded the Cathedral during its long history.

The present Dean was a Mr. Huntington, who had come from St. Patrick's Cathedral in New York.

Punkin took the marble staircase up to the third floor library. Upon entering, she saw the Charlesons, Suzie, and that distinguished gentleman with the eye patch she had said hello to at the American Club lunch. Standing over in a corner, looking quite small were three young women, all shapes and sizes and in various modes of dress. They looked nervous.

The dashing Frenchman, Jean Aumont, approached Punkin as she was getting a cup of coffee and a *croissant*.

"Hello again, I hope you remember me, Jean Aumont? We met at the American Club lunch."

"Yes, Monsieur Aumont, I remember. You have just come back to Paris from Algeria, *oui?*"

Punkin was a little nervous talking to this very handsome and very tall gentleman.

"Please, call me Jean. Yes, I have only been back in Paris for a few weeks. I am leaving soon to go to our family *chateau* in *Bordeaux*. The Aumonts have been making wine there for centuries."

"How interesting. I know France has some great vintages but do not know much about it."

"Perhaps we can have a *café* or a *coupe* soon. Are you available perhaps next week?"

Punkin grinned to herself, thinking, hey, another cute man maybe on the string. *Pourquoi pas*, why not?

"*Volontiers*, here is my *carte* with my telephone number. Just give me a call and we will set it up."

Suzie observed the two of them with their heads close together in conversation. When Punkin came back into the middle of the library to find a chair for the meeting, Suzie sidled up to her

"Well, you seem to have made a conquest there," she said

"Oh Suze, he seems quite nice," said Punkin

Tom invited everyone to take their coffees and take a seat so the meeting could begin.

"Thank you all for coming to this second meeting of the protégé program of the American Club. We thank Dean Huntington for the use of the library today."

Dean Huntington, a robust looking man of 70 with white longish hair, stood up and took a bow.

Eleanor continued the welcome.

"Tom and I consider this a very special project, one close to our hearts. I will introduce our young women, and then each can tell you a little about themselves."

"This is Simone Villar, age 19. She has enrolled in computer school and hopes to get a job working in social media."

Simone was small as a sparrow. She looked very much like Edith Piaf, in her dark dress and *beret*. She shyly stood up, bowed and sat back down without saying a word.

Eleanor tried to encourage her to speak, but to no avail, so she continued.

"This is Brigitte Bontemps, age 18. She has just come to us, and wants to finish her general schooling to get her *bac*/diploma. She would like to then enter the business world."

Brigitte, short and fat, with that French aquiline nose that seems to take up most of a face, stood up and curtsied. When she smiled, she showed a row of teeth that had probably never seen a dentist. Brigitte spoke haltingly in a very broken English.

"*Merci Madame* Eleanor. I happy to be here. Perhaps *quelqu'un* can help me. *Le bac* is very hard."

"Last but not least, this is Madeleine Junot, age 20. Madeleine was the first protégé recommended to us. She wishes to pursue a career as an artist. Tom and I have offered to help her."

Madeleine, who was almost as tall as Punkin, stood up. There was a kind of regal bearing about her, unlike the other girls. She was also dressed more flamboyantly. Her make-up was a bit garish. She had long, dark brown hair, almost black. It was shiny as ebony.

One could see there was a beautiful complexion under all that makeup, and she had an adorable little turned up nose. Some might have thought she looked like the actress Vivien Leigh. Her eyes were a deep azure blue. Punkin could not stop looking at them. They appeared sad, apprehensive, but also hopeful.

Madeleine spoke in a soft melodious voice, heavily accented like Brigitte's.

"*Bonjour*, I am Madeleine Junot, *enchante*. I thank *Madame* Eleanor and *Monsieur* Tom for helping me. My mother died when I was very young, and I went to live with relatives. I started drawing then and hope to make a career in art."

She stopped briefly, catching Punkin's eye. She tried to figure out what else to say.

"I have some samples of my work here."

She opened her portfolio, and passed it around. Madeleine observed that the group liked her efforts. Punkin was the most impressed of all.

"Perhaps you know *artiste* who might teach me, *oui?*"

That is all Punkin needed to hear. She stood right up.

"*Salut*, Madeleine. My name is Punkin Lowery. I think your work is *charmant* and shows promise. I have an artist friend who lives here and might take you as a student. He is an American from Louisiana. If you wish, I can set up a meeting for us."

'*C'est gentile, merci."*

They smiled at each other, each sizing the other up.

The rest of the meeting went on for about an hour with Simone and Brigitte talking to each American Club member, and pairing up with a sponsor. Suzie took "toothy" Brigitte. The tall elegant man from the American Club took sad Simone under his wing.

Madeleine and Punkin moved out into the hall to chat.

"Do you really think I have talent?"

"I am not an expert, but I know what I like. That drawing of the woman in particular is an excellent portrait. That is my favorite."

"That is how I remember my mother. I was only 5 when she died. She had the prettiest blond hair, like you *Madame* Punkin, and smelled of vanilla and lemon."

Madeleine said this with much emotion, and it touched Punkin.

"It must have been very hard losing your mother at such a young age. I just lost my mother who was my best friend. Even at my age, it has been *tres difficile*."

These two had something in common.

"How can I reach you?"

Madeleine looked a little squirmy. Punkin wondered if she couldn't afford a phone.

"It would be better if I call you. May I have your number?"

Punkin pulled out her organizer and her *carte de visite*, business card. She handed it to Madeleine. It had all her Paris details including her address. She thought nothing of giving the *carte* to Madeleine. It was a decision she would later regret.

Punkin was ready to get started with her protégé. A week later, she and Madeleine were at the *atelier* of Damien Hunter, her friend from college. He lived and worked in a 6th floor walk-up in *Montmartre*, near *Sacre Coeur*. The girls met on the street, and climbed the 7 flights of stairs to his door, arriving pretty breathless.

"I do get my exercise in ole Paree," huffed Punkin

"You will get used to it, *Madame*, I mean Punkin," said Madeleine

Damien flung open the door. His little dash hound, *Chou Chou*, was nipping at his heels, making the most horrific racket.

"Hi darlin' how are ya? Loving life in Paree?"

Damien retained all of his Louisiana accent, although he had been in Paris for many years.

He engulfed Punkin in his massive arms.

"Hi precious. Yes, I am living the dream. Thanks so much for agreeing to look at Madeleine's work."

"Madeleine, *je vous presente* Damien Hunter."

Madeleine timidly took his hand. She did not know him well enough for the 2-cheek kiss.

"*Bonjour Monsieur*"

Damien's apartment was a combination of living and working quarters. There was no delineation between the two. The expansive space, like a New York loft, was cluttered with clothes, canvases, wine bottles, and ashtrays filled with cigarette butts. Many of the canvases were portraits of young women, done in pastels. Some of them were nude.

Punkin's artist friend was tall and lean. He was 55, with salt and pepper hair which he wore long in the European way. He was easy on the eyes, but had no fashion sense. Today he was wearing a t-shirt speckled with old paint, torn jeans and cowboy boots.

Damien and Punkin had met at the University of Texas, and dated for a while. He had married his college sweetheart, but that had ended in divorce. Punkin didn't think his wife had moved to Paris with him some 20 years ago.

"Would y'all like a glass of wine? We can sit at the kitchen table and I can look at Madeleine's portfolio."

The kitchen was a bigger mess than the living room. The sink was filled with dirty dishes, and the kitchen table had glasses and plates left over from one meal or another. He began to review Madeleine's work.

"My first impression is that you have a natural gift. How long have you been drawing?"

"Since I was small. I cannot remember when I was not drawing. I told Punkin that after my mother died I went to live with my Aunt. She lives on the *Canal St. Martin*. I loved to watch the boats go up and down in the locks. I drew what I saw out of my window at the top of the house."

"These pictures have a sad quality. They are all in black and white. Why did you use no color?'

"Color crayons and paints are expensive. I couldn't afford them. *Donc*, I use mostly pen and ink. I would like for you to teach me, but I have no money to pay."

Madeleine said all this in a rushed, nervous way.

Punkin joined in the conversation.

"Dame, I was thinking, since you love to do portraits of young women, maybe Madeleine could model for you in exchange for lessons."

The light went off in Damien's head.

"That might work. I have several commissions for my landscapes, but I prefer to do portraits as you can see."

He pointed to the multiple canvases hanging on the wall.

"Would you be too shy to pose *au naturelle*?"

He looked at Madeleine and she returned his gaze with a wry smile, as if enjoying a private joke. In her profession she was NUDE most of the time.

"*Pas de probleme*. I think the human body is quite beautiful. We French are not ashamed of our bodies."

Punkin was pleased and said,

"You too seem to have hit it off!"

"Hit what?"

Madeleine had a quizzical look.

"Oh I keep forgetting. This is American slang. It means you two seem *sympa*."

"Can you start tomorrow? I always say no time like the present," said Damien

Madeleine had that same edgy look that she displayed at the meeting.

"I must see. I have several commitments *demain*."

"Ok, here is my number. Just give me a call since I am always here."

Punkin and Madeleine left Damien's and kissed good-bye on the street. They each headed into their own direction. Punkin got on her bus back to the *centre ville*, and Madeleine descended into the metro to go the opposite direction to *St. Denis*.

CHAPTER 9

Romance Beckons on a Ride in the Bois de Boulogne

Punkin was very happy that Jean Aumont talked to her and invited her for a drink at the protégé meeting. Sure enough, a couple of days after the meeting at the beginning of the next week, they met for a glass of wine at *Café Deux Magots*. They talked a lot about wine, and Punkin observed Jean was serious about his profession. They also discovered they both loved horses and riding. Texan Punkin had grown up in the saddle, and even had a horse at one time on Daddy T's ranch.

She was pleasantly surprised to get a call from him just a day after their date, inviting her for a ride. He was a member of the exclusive *Polo de Paris*, the private country club in the *Bois de Boulogne*. It had a polo field, stables, and a clubhouse. The *Bois,* one of the largest parks in Paris, had many riding trails.

They made a date to meet, but their first effort was rained out. The wind and rain in Paris in the fall and winter could be severe. Punkin could not believe how fast time was passing. Thanksgiving and her *grand dejeuner* for her neighbors and friends was less than a month away.

Their second try was more successful. The day dawned cool and sunny. It was a perfect day for a ride. Punkin had brought her jodhpurs, boots, and riding helmet from the US. She took the bus to the *Bois,* and arrived at 11am. Jean met her at the members-only entrance.

He was 6 feet 4" tall. Punkin loved tall men. Being so tall herself, it was hard to find a man that towered over her. His black hair was cropped short in a military cut, graying at the temples. The eye patch covered his right eye but his left was a pale corn flower blue. It crinkled when he smiled. He had a ruddy complexion from all his years in the sun in Algeria. He was impeccably dressed for the ride. His boots were polished to a high sheen, reflecting like a mirror. Punkin guessed he was near her age.

"*Bonjour Mademoiselle, comment allez- vous?*"

"*Tres bien et vous- meme?*"

"*Ca va*"

That kind of meant he was having a so- so day. Jean seemed more reserved and aloof than at their first meeting. He kind of reminded her of Alex. She hoped to elevate his mood. The two walked to the stables adjacent to the swimming pool. How amusing, Punkin thought. It was never warm enough in Paris to swim except maybe in July and August.

Jean had picked out a gentle mare for her to ride, about 15 hands high. She was relieved she did not have to make a grand stretch to mount her horse. Jean would be riding his regular mount, a black stallion. As thy started out on the ride, they began to converse.

"I so enjoyed our drink the other night. Your life at the chateau sounds magical," she said as they bumped down the road.

"It is a beautiful place, built in the 17th century. You will have to visit sometime. We have a stable full of horses and it is wonderful to ride amidst the vines."

Oooh good, Punkin thought. He was already considering a third date.

"When we met at the protégé meeting I wasn't sure you had remembered me."

"*Bien sur*, I always remember pretty women."

Punkin blushed under her helmet, and changed the subject.

"I understand you knew Suzie before at the Club. She told me that your grandfather was on *de Gaulle*'s staff during the war. The general is one of my heroes."

"*C'est vrai*. My grandfather, *Etienne*, was with *de Gaulle* when he fled to England. They came back for the glorious liberation of Paris in '44."

"I love the history of World War II. My dad was in the war, but stationed in the US. Do you know the book 'Is Paris Burning'?"

"*Certainement*, but I am surprised you do. It was written in 1962, and has been out of print for years."

"Don't remember how I found it. It is fascinating since it is a true story. Everything could have gone so wrong and the bombs set under all the bridges and monuments detonated. Apparently Hitler knew he was losing the war and wanted Paris in rubbles."

Jean could not get a word in edgewise when Punkin was on a roll.

"My mother tells me it was a horrific four years of occupation. She has terrible memories of the cold, and no food or heat. There was not even enough leather for shoes. The women took to wearing *sabots*, wooden shoes, like you see in Holland."

"We Americans have no concept of living in an occupied country. I think the French were quite brave to get on as well as they did. I still get chills when I see the old newsreels of the Nazi's marching into Paris in 1940. Was your mother actually in Paris during the war?"

"Yes, she was a young girl of 12 going to convent school in Paris. Her parents and little brother lived in the family chateau in *Bordeaux*. Luckily, the Germans let them keep it, because they loved drinking the chateau's outstanding vintages. My mother stayed in Paris during the week and then took the train to *Bordeaux* for the weekends. Thankfully, the chateau was a working farm so they didn't starve like many others."

"A girl of 12 is pretty young to be left alone in Paris, in my opinion."

She hoped she was not offending Jean when she said it.

"The sisters took good care of her. She did tell me that one had to be careful even as a young child, if caught after curfew. The

German soldiers had the right to shoot on sight. If a German officer had been killed on a particular day, the soldiers would indiscriminately shoot those coming out of the metro and theatres in retaliation. It was an awful time. Now, France and Germany are allies."

"I guess time heals. It is so interesting to me that so many people who experienced the occupation are still alive. They are living history," said Punkin

"There are many left, indeed. I will tell you a story of what happened to my mother. She and my uncle, who was only 10 at the time, were taking the train from Paris to *Bordeaux*. He had come up to visit her. It was a moon- lit night, and my mother remembered that the Allies always bombed on clear nights when the moon was full. The train stopped in a small town near *Cognac*. For some reason, she had a premonition that she and her brother should get off the train. They quickly jumped off and ran into the woods. Five minutes later, the bombs began to fall and the train and station blew up like matchsticks."

"*Incroyable*, hard to believe."

"Since you are so interested in the war's history, perhaps you would like to meet my mother, *Giselle*. She stays at the chateau, rarely coming to Paris."

"What a nice invitation. It would be a pleasure to meet your mother and visit the chateau."

They rode for another 30 minutes, galloping, trotting, and going over jumps. Punkin loved it. Jean told Punkin more about himself. She was surprised he was getting so 'intimate" so fast. Most French people were so reserved. He said he had been madly in love when he was 18 with a young Parisian girl and had never gotten over it. The relationship had ended abruptly and without reason when he left for Algeria. He had married there, but this other woman, Rose. had been the love of his life.

For once, Punkin was quiet about her love life. She wasn't quite ready to tell Jean about Alex and his suicide. He might also think it strange that she had never married. When he asked her about her romantic life, she side-stepped a bit, saying only that she had had her romances, but her career had been all consuming.

CHAPTER 10

All the News That's Fit to Print

Punkin's life was moving at a fast pace. She and Suzie Gilmore had become running buddies and often went for long lunches in the best French tradition. They loved to go out at night and dance at *La Coupole* on *Blvd Montparnasse* with the young gigolos, always looking for a rich, older woman to take care of them.

Punkin had not seen Suzie since the Charleson's bridge party. She was busy with her kids and her little protégé Brigitte from the American Club. With a potential new boyfriend in Jean Aumont, the continuation of her affair with Sebastian and her work with protégé, Madeleine, she was happily busy, too. Plus, she was in the midst of finalizing plans for the Thanksgiving lunch. She had so much news to tell Suzie.

They made a date to meet at one of their favorite places, *Les Ministeres*, a wonderful *belle epoque* style restaurant on *rue de bac*, not far from Suzie's apartment. It was famous for its oysters from Normandy. They tasted like they just came out of the sea. The house champagne wasn't bad either.

Suzie arrived before Punkin and was seated at one of the *banquettes*. She looked fetching in her long brown leather coat which matched the color of the *banquette* perfectly. A *beret* sprinkled with sequins was perched at a charming angle on her blond head.

"Hey there, sister" Punkin greeted her with a double-cheek kiss.

"*Salut, mon amie.* Just ordered a *coupe de champagne* for both of us. I hope you are not in a hurry. I want to hear all your news, " said Suzie

Punkin was pretty content with herself, and it must have shown. She tried to curb her enthusiasm and talk in quiet tones. She had such a booming voice, and had done some singing in her day. The one thing in Paris that distinguished ex-pat Americans form the French is that they talked so loud. Many times when Punkin was on the bus and talking on her cell phone, many a disgruntled "Frog" gave her a dirty look. She was "disturbing the peace" of the bus.

"First, let me tell you about Sebastian. I am so happy to be having SEX again. It's true, like riding a bicycle, you never forget."

"You go girl. That is ten times better than dancing with those boys at *La Coupole*. I can't imagine sleeping with one of them," Suzie said with a grimace.

"Sebastian is a terrific lover and very sensitive."

"How often do you get to see him? I know he is married."

"Actually, pretty often. His work schedule is very flexible. He even took me to one of his film shoots. It was quite interesting."

"This pm we are planning a little *cinq a sept.*"

Punkin loved this term for afternoon trysts by French lovers, usually in the afternoons between 5 and 7pm.

"Can you separate sex from love? I think that is hard for a woman. If you can do it, more power to you."

"It is a struggle, but I know there is no future with Sebastian so I have been looking elsewhere. You remember Jean Aumont?"

"Get out! You haven't been seeing him, too?"

"We have had TWO dates already. Our second date was a for a ride in the *Bois*, from the exclusive *Polo de Paris*. This guy is a real 'aristo' and someone I could really get interested in."

"Remember what I told you about Frenchmen and their mothers. Most of these guys are spoiled rotten. I told you his mother is supposed to be a real imperious bitch."

Punkin laughed. She loved Suzie's straightforward way of putting things.

"We will cross that bridge when we come to it. However, he has mentioned my visiting their chateau and meeting his mother."

"Wow, he must have designs on you to offer that invitation so quickly."

"We will see."

The waiter brought the menus and the girls indeed ordered the oysters with a *carafe* of good *Chablis*.

"On another subject, how is your little 'prossie' Madeleine?"

"Oh Suzie, I don't think she is a real prostitute. My artist buddy Damien, thinks she has a lot of talent. He says she might amount to something as an *artiste*."

"Who is Damien? You have not mentioned him before."

"A darling former boyfriend from Louisiana who has lived here for over 20 years. Now there might be someone for you!"

"Not really interested until my divorce comes through, but tell me more."

"Damien has offered to give Madeleine art lessons in exchange for her modeling for one of his portraits."

"Oooh, should we say a little 'hanky panky'?"

"Girl, how you do go on. Damien is a righteous dude and I trust him."

"OK, but continuing about Madeleine, what about that pimp?"

Suzie was not letting go of the subject.

"Madeleine has told me a little about him. I think she mainly sleeps with him, not a lot of other customers. His name is Marcel and he sounds creepy."

"Who would have thought two genteel Southern girls would be talking about a pimp?" Suzie took a big slurp of an oyster and swallowed it down and continued.

"What if Marcel comes after you? He doesn't know where you live does he?"

That is when Punkin remembered about her *carte* that she had given to Madeleine.

"Gee, I hope not, especially since I am thinking about asking Madeleine to move in with me."

Suzie gasped, knocking over her glass of wine. It went all over the table and scattered the bowl of peanuts which crashed to the floor. While the waiter was moping it all up, she said.

"Are you out of your mind? Asking a strange girl in the world's oldest profession to live in your beautiful apartment? What it she tried to stab you in the middle of the night and take all your jewelry and money?"

"Suze, you watch too many movies. Madeleine and I have been spending a lot of time together, going to museums and out to eat. I think I am a pretty good judge of character. I would not purposely put myself in harm's way".

"Just the same, I think you should ponder this decision a little longer. You can help her without her living with you."

"I am just thinking about it. Maurice and I just rattle around that big apartment, and Madeleine has kind of become my *cause celebre*."

The girls got more wine and ordered another dozen *fins de Claire* oysters.

Suzie was getting to know Punkin quite well. She knew her new best friend could be stubborn and not prone to suggestions. Suzie, wanting to continue with a pleasant lunch, changed the subject.

"I am really looking forward to your Thanksgiving lunch," she said

"I am having so much fun planning it. I have asked my neighbors, plus you and the Charlesons and even Sebastian and his wife."

"Boy, you like to live dangerously," said Suzie as she slurped another oyster.

"I am even inviting Jean. He has promised to bring bottles of his family's famous *Aumont cru*."

"What can I bring?"

"Just yourself, honey chile. I would invite the kids but this is more of an adult party."

"That's ok, since Thanksgiving is on a Thursday, the kids will be in school. It is not a holiday here like in our country."

The girls passed an agreeable afternoon eating and drinking. Punkin didn't tell her friend that she was concerned about getting too close to Madeleine. She was seeing Sebastian in about an hour and wanted his point of view.

CHAPTER 11

A Divinity, but a Handful

Punkin was having some troubles with Madeleine. She did like mothering the girl, but Madeleine could be petulant and difficult at times. She had such mood swings, some violent in nature. She did worry about her moving in. Punkin was making progress in befriending this girl and building an element of trust, but she still would not give Punkin her cell number. She had a heart-wrenching suspicion that Madeleine was continuing to live with Marcel.

What Punkin told Suzie was true. She had been spending a lot of time with Madeleine. Madeleine knew so much about art that she was like a little tour guide at the museums. Punkin could make her laugh and lighten her dark moods. However, she began to notice disturbing things in Madeleine. There were little bruises on her upper arms, and this beautiful girl sometimes had dark circles under her eyes meaning she was not getting enough sleep. One time at lunch, Madeleine fell asleep at the table. She did eat heartily when she was with Punkin but she was extremely thin.

Trust was developing between the two, which was a big step dealing with a young girl who had felt abandoned all her life. But, it was frustrating because she could not pull the whole story of her childhood out of Madeleine. She must take "baby steps", she told herself.

On the Marcel issue, she would ask the advice of Sebastian and her dear neighbor George Castellane. He was Sebastian's brother-in-law and a noted attorney. He would tell Punkin what the legal ramifications might be if she did ask this waif to move in.

The divinity was a handful.

CHAPTER 12

Neighbors

Voisines/Voisins

Some of the neighbors in Punkin's building on *Avenue President Wilson* would be at the Thanksgiving lunch. She had never taken the time to regale Suzie about them, but they were a very complex bunch. The building only had 5 floors, with one neighbor per floor. Her floor was the exception because as noted, her apartment had been part of a larger one on the 5th floor.

Sebastian's in-laws, the Castellanes, lived next door to her. George Castellane Sr. was a successful publisher but his wife Ingride had more money. She was the heiress to a communication company in Vienna. The Castellanes' apartment was over 3,000 square feet. They did not however have as good a view of the Tower.

The top floor, which was the 6th, was vacant and used for storage. These small rooms called *chambres des bonnes*, were servant's quarters in the 19th and early 20th century. The cramped spaces were boiling in the summer and freezing in the winter with only one small window for ventilation.

On the 4th floor, were *Monsieur et Madame* Segretti. Husband Mario was Italian and his wife, Chantal, was French. Their daughter, Claudine, was a prima ballerina at the *Opera Garnier*. Chantal was much younger than Mario, and there was talk in the building that she was having an affair with the French Prime Minister.

Located on the 3rd floor was the mystery man. No one ever saw him, but the story was that he lived in Berlin, and only used his large Paris apartment as a *pied a terre*. He was in a wheelchair, and that is why the *co-proprietes*, other owners, had voted to install a huge glass elevator between the staircase, since he agreed to pay for most of it.

On the *etage noble*, 2nd floor, lived the two widows, *Madame de la Fontaine* and *Madame Jonville*. They shared *Madame Fontaine's* huge 5,000 square foot apartment magnificently appointed in 18th century antiques. Adele, a widow for over 40 years, acted more youthful than her age. She still ran her husband's successful insurance company, and had the distinction of being a member of the *Legion d'honneur*. She wore her red rosette proudly. Estelle, *Madame Jonville*, was in her late 60's and recently widowed. Her husband, *Pascale*, had been in the Foreign Service and they had lived all over the world, his last posting being in Beirut. She lived in a tiny part of the apartment cordoned off by a red curtain at the entry. She was trying to live on her husband's meager pension. Adele and Estelle became grand pals of Punkin and invited her to the apartment often for festive dinners where they helped her practice her French.

The *voisin* on the 1st floor was the Castellanes' son, George, Jr. He was in his early 30's, practiced law and appeared older both in dress and demeanor. He was always dressed in a coat and tie no matter what day of the week. He and Punkin had become real buddies. Through the recommendation of his parents, and Sebastian, he had become her attorney. They spent many an enjoyable evening in his apartment drinking champagne and dancing to American Rock 'n Roll.

Last but not least on the *rez de chaussee*, ground floor, lived Catherine the *gardienne*, her husband *Jerome*, and little baby *Francois*. They occupied the *loge*, a very small apartment given to each *gardienne* of a building by the owners. She was only 25, very young for a superintendent of such a prestigious building. Husband Jerome worked for the *SNCF*, national rail service. Their two salaries combined couldn't have been much, but they had 2 cars and a vacation home in Normandy. Punkin could never figure that out.

She was happy with her neighbors but was glad there weren't too many of them.

CHAPTER 13

Sebastian gives advice

Punkin did not get home from her lunch with Suzie until after 4pm. Sebastian was arriving at 5. She took Maurice for a short walk and then slipped on an ice-blue teddy and poured on the perfume. The weather continued to be wintry so she lit a fire. The apartment glowed with warmth and coziness. She opened a bottle of champagne and placed it in a bucket near the sofa. Sebastian never liked to do it on the bed.

He arrived promptly at 5pm and barely looked at her sexy attire before he had it off. After making love, she offered him a glass of champagne and they snuggled in the duvet. She began to talk about Madeleine.

"*Cherie*, as long as I have your undivided attention, I want your advice on something from a man's point of view."

She snuggled closer to Sebastian and gave him a kiss on the cheek.

"What is it, *ma petite chou?*"

Calling your loved one a little cabbage was a term of endearment in French.

"You know I have mentioned to you my little protégé Madeleine."

"*Oui*, you said she has quite the talent as an *artiste*."

He wrapped his arms and legs around her, giving her a sip of his champagne.

"My artist friend thinks so, but there could be a problem."

There was no other way to say it but just say it.

"She has a pimp."

There, *ca fait*, it was out in the open.

Sebastian shot up from his comfortable position.

"*Mon dieu*"

"Apparently she has been working out in *St. Denis*, and this guy keeps dragging her back into the life. It is kind of like she takes one positive step forward and two negative steps back."

"What is your question?"

"Do you think my association with her might put me at risk?"

"That is a tough one. Do you think she has told him anything about you?"

"Obviously, I have asked her not to, but who knows what she does when she is not with me? I do know his name is Marcel, and how she has described him is positively terrifying."

"Are you seeing her again soon?"

"We are going to lunch next week and maybe I can get some more information. I have a powerful intuition about this girl. I am sure she can be helped. I am even thinking about asking her to move in with me."

Sebastian got quiet for a moment.

"Selfishly speaking, *mon ange*, if she does move in, our little *rendez-vous* will not be as easy to arrange. Have you thought it might make it worse with her pimp if she leaves him and moves in with you? What if the guy shows up here!"

Punkin had not thought of that. It was a valid point. That could be a nightmare.

Sebastian buried his head back in the duvet and pulled her close. He was ready to make love again. At 7pm, he was dressed and out the door, leaving Punkin with her dilemma.

CHAPTER 14

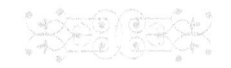

Marcel the Pimp and a Decision

Paris, November 9, 2000

I am beginning to think Sebastian is a major dick! He just doesn't want me to have Madeleine living here because it will spoil his "sex romps". I am kind of getting tired of being treated like the welcome wagon anytime he wants to show up. Plus, now that I am getting to know Jean better, I want to take that relationship further. I have never been able to sleep with two guys at the same time so one has got to go and that will be Sebastian, I know in my heart of hearts.

Seeing Madeleine today. That is always a pleasure. Just have to take that leap of faith and go on my intuition about her. Yes, Marcel is a problem, but what relationship that had any worth did NOT have some problems or obstacles?

Getting excited about Thanksgiving. I have yeses from 14 people, including Jean. What a really nice guy he is. I hope he will be as good in the sack and have large 'equipment' like Sebastian! Did I say that? Only to my journal."

Punkin was tickled pink that Madeleine and Damien were getting along so well. She was working as his model, and he had begun a stunning portrait of her. The news on her artistic progress was excellent. They were now in constant contact. Madeleine would call her everyday around 10am and they would make plans. They had progressed from seeing each other once a week to now almost every day. Madeleine was still a little reserved, but Punkin's great capacity for love was wearing her down. Madeleine allowed Punkin to hug her at times. She tried to encourage her artistic abilities, and make her feel she had much self-worth.

After talking to Sebastian, Punkin needed to make a decision. She guessed, like everything in her life, the answer would come. It was giving her some sleepless nights. She invited Madeleine to lunch at the *Café Marly* in the Louvre for a treat and a good talk. It was an expensive place. Punkin had been spending a lot of money lately, and the lunch would be very expensive. Her bank balance was going down pretty fast. She might have to get a job, at least part time. But she wouldn't think about that today. Today she would enjoy her lunch with Madeleine.

November was here. It was sunny but cold. The *Café Marly* was in the colonnade of the Louvre with a lovely terrace facing the pyramid. They sat down at a table on the terrace, and the bright sunshine warmed them.

Madeleine seemed troubled this day. She began to talk more about Marcel with no prompting from Punkin. She described him as being around 30, with piercing black eyes and a shock of black hair which he gelled up into a spike. She said he always wore leather jeans, a black leather biker jacket, and heavy hob-nail boots. He had a habit of rolling an old French *franc* piece between his fingers when he was nervous. She knew when he started to do that, she was in for a beating. She was either not bringing in enough money, or tricking for the same tired clientele. That may have explained the tiny bruises that Punkin has noticed on her upper arms.

Marcel's turf was the streets of *St. Denis*. He had grown up in this grimy area, located north of the city near the *Stade de France*, soccer stadium. The suburb had once been a glorious place. The 16th century Cathedral still loomed large in the middle of this dreary town. Many kings of France were buried there. In this century, however, one shouldn't go into *St. Denis* even during the day. It was a hangout for drug dealers, illegal North Africans and all kinds of social debris.

The big question looming in the air like a cartoon balloon was-Did Marcel know about Punkin? It took most of the long lunch to get this information. It appeared Marcel had stolen Madeleine's purse, which had Punkin's business card in it. So, he knew where she lived and how to contact her. (At least he didn't have the building code to get in)

Good Lord, Punkin got a momentary chill. What was she doing in this situation? This young girl was not her blood relative. Why be the patsy? But then she thought rather quickly, one life touches another. As the Christian religion taught, one should be a good Samaritan and help their fellow man. How could Punkin turn her back on this defenseless, homeless girl?

They finished lunch and Madeleine was still agitated about Marcel. She didn't have any new bruises but his psychological hold on her was immense. To cheer her up, Punkin asked her to come along on the shopping spree for the Thanksgiving lunch. The went into *Le Marais* to the restaurant Thanksgiving where they picked out a 14-pound turkey which Punkin would dress and cook herself. The owner of Thanksgiving offered a *maître d'hotel* at a small additional charge to finish the cooking and serve during the cocktail hour.

On the bus back to *President Wilson* the two chattered away like best friends. Punkin had not told Madeleine that she had arranged for the American Club to do a *vernissage*, exhibition of Damien's work, right before Thanksgiving. Her portrait would be on display with his other works.

Once they got back to the apartment, everything just fell into place. Madeleine said again how much she loved being there and bingo, the decision was made. She asked Maddie, as she was now calling her, to move in. Was she crazy? She just went with her gut.

"So, Maddie, what do you think?"

"I am surprised. Are you sure? I think it would be *merveilleuse* to live together."

Punkin kissed her, and Madeleine hugged her so tight, it took her breath away. They fixed the move- in date for the week of the *vernissage*. That way she would be settled before Thanksgiving. She would be a big help to Punkin during the gala lunch.

Madeleine left to go tell her Aunt she was moving out. Punkin wondered how she would tell Marcel, but she wouldn't think about that today. She poured herself a glass of wine and went into the living room to gaze at the Tower. The sun was just setting and gave the Tower a deep ruby glow. Little Maurice followed her and she said to him,

"Looks like *toi et moi* are going to have a roommate. Would you like that?

Maurice barked his voice of approval.

Paris was becoming home. Madeleine moving in would help end the Sebastian affair. She was going to concentrate more effort in getting to know Jean Aumont. As she finished her wine, she realized she had no reason to go back to America. Everything was working out in this celebratory time of the year.

CHAPTER 15

A Grim World

Madeleine had said she was off to tell her Aunt she was moving, which was a bit of a lie. She was really going back into the bowels of *St. Denis* to face Marcel. Punkin knew that she had moved in with her Aunt when her mother died. What she didn't know was that before that, she had lived with her grand-parents until she was 10. Her grand-parents looked on her with disdain because she was a born out of wedlock. They considered her a bastard even though she was their flesh and blood. They died in quick succession of each other, and that is when she went to live with *Tante Celeste*.

Her Aunt was a sour woman. She was not very attractive always being overweight. No man had ever asked her to be his. Spinster Celeste was mad at life because it had passed her by. She thought she was being put upon once again to take responsibility for this small child. It was just another way life was hitting her in the face. She put Madeleine in a tiny room at the top of her house on *Canal St. Martin*. Like a *chambre de bonne*, the room was always too hot or too cold and there was little fresh air. She was left alone all the time, and her art and imagination were her only consolations. As she matured and become more beautiful, her Aunt hated her more.

She met Marcel at age 16. He seemed charming and so strong. She had never had a father to guide her, and Marcel's compliments and encouragement appealed to her. Someone actually liked her! He asked her to move in, and then everything changed. She was a virgin, and he brutally raped her. He told her repeatedly that she would have to get used to abuse from him and earn money for them both by having sex with nameless, faceless men.

Shock gradually gave way to acceptance. She had no place else to go. Her life became an endless series of assignations, sometimes four a day. She went deep into herself while sweaty, smelly men groaned and moved on top of her.

All seemed hopeless until the "ray of light" that was the protégé program and Punkin Lowery. This glimmer of a better life gave her resolve. Punkin had made her a miraculous offer, and she was returning to Marcel one last time to say it was *finis*.

They lived in a cramped apartment only 200 square feet, at the top of a crumbling building near the Cathedral. Their building smelled of stale cabbage and sausages cooking in old grease. She had tried to make their room as comfortable as possible. It did have a view on the Cathedral and when the weather was good, the sun shone on its spires. She had begun a painting of it.

She returned from Punkin's apartment, her new home, to find Marcel watching soccer on TV. He was drinking a beer and seemed quite intoxicated. A *pot au feu*, beef stew, was cooking on their one electric cook top. When she entered, he barely acknowledged her.

"*Eh bien*, so where have you been?"

Marcel looked at her with a menacing grin, showing a row of bad teeth. Madeleine sat down across from him, far enough away so he could not reach her.

"I have been with my new friend, *Madame* Lowery. I have something to tell you."

She said in a timorous voice, shaking on the inside.

"Oh that rich American bitch. I hope she is not filling your head with any grand ideas. Maybe we can get some money out of her. Remember, you are mine, and I plan to keep you until you are no longer any use to me."

He reached for her hand, but she pulled away. In a flash, all the courage she had in her soul emerged. She was almost shouting.

"I am not yours, and *c'est fini*, this is over! I am leaving today and will never return."

Marcel had never detected such a decisive tone in Madeleine and the surprise left him temporarily at a loss for words. He blinked, anger rising in his eyes. He stood up and lunged at her.

"On no, *ma Cherie*, you will never leave me, unless I kill you!"

She jumped out of his way and back towards the tiny kitchen. All she saw at that moment was the large casserole cooking on the stove. She grabbed its handle, burning her hand badly. She threw the steaming stew in his face. He grabbed his eyes and screamed.

"You, *putaine*."

Dazed by the heat and burning of the stew, he lost his balance and fell to the floor. It was just enough time for Madeleine to grab her suitcase and art supplies she had already packed. She did not look back at Marcel as she slammed the door behind her.

CHAPTER 16

Le Vernissage

It was two days before the grand exposition at the American Club. Punkin had worked hard on this project, reaching out to all the Club members and making sure it would be a spectacular evening. This was her big chance to shine before the social elite of Paris. She was also anticipating Madeleine's immediate move- in.

Everything was ordered for Thanksgiving and she was excited about the holiday. She was a bit concerned that she had not heard from Madeleine today. Perhaps she was still at her Aunt's? She shuddered to think how or if she had told Marcel she was leaving him. She did not have the phone number of her Aunt.

Punkin's anxiety levels had dropped since moving to Paris and being happy. Now, those old nagging feelings were coming back. She had to control herself. That evening she and little Maurice paced the floor and she slept fitfully.

The next morning, she decided to let it go. She had to concentrate on the *vernissage*. Working on that would take her mind off Madeleine. The event was this evening and even Jean's mother *Giselle* would be there. It turned out that her neighbor, *Adele de la Fontaine* knew *Giselle Aumont*. They had gone to school together. *Adele* told Punkin that after the war, *Giselle* married a man from a neighboring wine family, and Jean was their only child. After her husband's death, she continued to run the business, and was determined that Jean would take over now that he had retired from the military. *Adele* liked *Giselle* very much. Punkin hoped she would, too.

Jean has been teaching Punkin a lot about wine. She knew that *Bordeaux* is one of the two leading wine-making regions of France, and is located in southwestern France. The other leading region Jean told her about is Burgundy in southeastern France. The big difference between the two she came to think was that the *vignerons* of Burgundy cultivated their grapes on much smaller parcels of land. In *Bordeaux,* the vineyards are anchored by huge manor houses and *chateaux* normally in the center of the property. Punkin liked the wines of both regions but thought she might like the Burgundians better. They seemed to have a harder task, to make great wine on very few acres.

She wondered what Jean's mother might think of her. She had several American friends who were married to French men, and they all said the same thing. Their mother's in law doted on their sons, and if anything went wrong in the marriage, it was always the woman's fault. If the woman was American, that made it worse.

The evening of the *vernissage* the weather turned perfect. It was about 45 degrees, clear skies and no rain, which would guarantee a big turn- out. Both Damien and Punkin arrived at the American Club at the same time. Damien wanted to put the finishing touches on his installation, and Punkin need to be *a l'heure*, on time, to meet and greet.

She was dressed to the nines in all her French finery. Tonight was the perfect time for her full length mink coat, her *Yves St. Laurent* black sheath, and her *Chanel* earrings, handbag and shoes. She had completed her outfit with her mother's lustrous pearls.

"Hi Dame"

"Hi P. You look *tres chic*."

"You look good enough to eat your own self. I have never seen you in a suit."

Punkin was reverting back to a strong Texas accent. She lapsed into it when speaking with other Americans, especially Southerners. Damien did look quite appealing. He had brought a good cross- section of his work which included the portrait of Madeleine. Punkin had not seen it before, and it was prominently displayed at the entrance to the exposition space.

"Wow, I love the Madeleine portrait. I think you have really captured her beauty and fragility."

The portrait was not a nude, but done in the style of John Singer Sergeant. Madeleine was robed in a black velvet dress that perfectly accented her ebony hair and azure blue eyes.

"She is easy to look at. That is for sure. She was so patient in posing. The portrait took me longer than most. I had to get the dress texture, and her hair and complexion just right. Maybe someone will buy it. Little *Choo Choo* and I need the dough ree mee."

"I am sure our well- heeled members will cough up some cash for your work *ce soir*."

"Is Madeleine coming? I have not heard from her in a week," added Damien

"Oh dear, sorry to hear that. I have not heard from her either. She is supposed to be moving in with me this week."

"Moving in? That is a big step. When did you decide that?"

"Madeleine and I cooked it up some weeks ago. I get so lonely in that big apartment, and she needs a more stable environment."

"Gad, she is a gorgeous girl, and doing so well in her lessons. I might be able to get her into *Les Ecoles de Beaux Arts*."

"Wow, you think she is that good?"

"Yes, I do."

Since the guests were not arriving for another quarter hour, the two continued to talk.

"Has she told you much about her life?" Punkin said

"Just that she is trying to start a new one. I do know about the pimp. Awful, ain't it?"

"Pretty bad. Selfishly, I hope her sordid life does not spill over into mine."

"You know I love you Punkin, so just be careful." Damien's face registered a look as if Punkin was making a big mistake.

"I am sure it will work out fine. She is helping me with the Thanksgiving lunch. You are coming aren't you?"

"Wouldn't miss it for the world. Do I have to wear a suit again?"

Punkin laughed.

"Yes, you do. And I have someone I want you to meet tonight. Suzie Gilmore is a knock-out, and single."

"Ugh, I am not real fond of fix-ups," Damien said as he saw guests arriving into the ballroom. He beat a hasty retreat back to his installation which was in an adjoining room.

The first people to arrive were Tom and Eleanor.

"Bonsoir mes amies, comment va-tu?"

"Hello darling girl. This was a great idea. We might just put you on the Board if you can come up with more events like this," said Tom

"How did you find the time to organize this and your lunch?" Eleanor said

"*Oui*, I am a bit tired. There are too many things going on at the same time. The Thanksgiving lunch planning is almost done, but now I must get the apartment ready for Madeleine's move-in."

Eleanor looked at Punkin as if she had lost her mind.

"You are letting that prostitute move in with you?"

She emphasized the word to great effect.

Punkin was tired of Eleanor's stuck up ways. She fired back with both barrels.

"Eleanor, I do not want to offend, but who made you God?"

Eleanor could see our Texas girl meant business and backed down a little. Tom was steadying her arm, signaling this was neither the time nor the place to get into a cat fight.

"Well, I mean, it is just a surprise. You are the only person who thinks Madeleine is any good."

With that remark, she dragged Tom away to the bar.

Punkin also wanted a drink, but she waited until the Charlesons had left the bar before she went over herself. By chance, Jean and his mother was standing there. They must have come in while she was talking to the Charlesons. At first glance, Punkin thought Giselle did not look her 80 years of age. It was not cosmetic work, but her aura of class. She had steel gray hair which was elegantly coiffed in a chignon, and wasn't wearing much jewelry. Her clothes were perfectly tailored, probably couture. Her eyes were the same corn silk blue as

Jean's. She looked like a bolt of fine *Duchesse* satin, all smooth, soft and shiny.

Jean greeted Punkin warmly and introduced her to his mother.

"*Enchante*," Punkin said as she extended her hand.

Giselle looked her up and down in a quick moment. She weakly took Punkin's hand and then released it quickly.

"Happy to meet you."

Giselle spoke perfect English, albeit with a British accent. Punkin guessed that her training at the convent school had been by Anglo-Saxton speaking nuns. That was usually the case on the Continent. Punkin was happy that she did not have to think in French to compete with her.

"Jean tells me you are an American from Texas."

"That's right, but I feel I am home in Paris. I truly love everything about this country," Punkin said as she smiled in Jean's direction.

"There are too many Americans here in my opinion. You all started coming after the war. I would think your country would have more advantages for you than France," Giselle huffed.

"*Peut-etre*, perhaps, but we do not have the *Tour Eiffel* or the *Arc de Triomphe*," she said trying to be amusing.

Giselle was going to be a tough crowd, so she tried again.

"I find the French so much more *cultive* than my countrymen. I think they are more honest in some ways, too."

Silence from Giselle and Jean had a pained look. She realized she was getting nowhere so she excused herself to return to the front entrance. Thankfully, the next person she saw was dear Suzie.

"The cavalry has arrived," she said giving Suzie a huge hug.

"What?"

"You just rescued me from a tense situation. I just met Jean's mother."

'Uh, oh, take that in stride. French women are all jealous of American women anyway. They assume we are all rich."

"Thanks, sister, I can always count on you to buck me up."

Suzie was looking around the room to see who was there.

"Where is this fabulous *artiste*? I am dying to meet Damien Hunter.

She looked smashing. She was dressed in a *costume smoking*, tuxedo jacket with black satin pants. She had no shirt on under the jacket and her ample bosom was on display.

"I will introduce you shortly. I am sure you will get along famously. You could charm a possum out of its hole."

The girls laughed. They both loved those old Southern expressions.

"Is Madeleine coming tonight?"

"Damien asked the same thing. I was just telling him I haven't heard from her, and it worries me. I did ask her to move in with me."

"What made you do a stupid thing like that?"

Suzie looked a little put out with her friend.

"*Et tu Brute*? Eleanor just said the same thing. I wanted to wring that chicken neck of hers."

"Oh good, some drama," Suzie said rubbing her hands together in delight.

"No drama. You all need to realize as my friends that I am really attached to this girl. She is kind of like the daughter I never had."

"Yeah, except a daughter with a pimp. We have giving you our opinions, but it is your life."

Punkin said *bienvenue* to more of the Club members, and surveyed the scene of her triumph. She could see Damien across the hall talking with animation, and selling his works like hotcakes. The portrait of Madeleine was getting the most attention. Her mind was on Madeleine. Would she have to go down into the garbage can of *St. Denis* to rescue her?"

CHAPTER 17

A Discovery on Moving Day

Paris, November 22, 2000

"Quelle nuit! A Triumph, bien sur, but Jean's mother, ooh la-là. I think the bitch hated me. Oh well, she doesn't know that Jean and I are getting closer- Tant pis- too bad for her. Last weekend was fabulous in Normandy. I was surprised he asked me to go away with him. I was a little nervous, but all turned out better than I imagined. We stayed in the sweetest little chateau hotel. Making love was so natural. He is a strong and a very athletic lover. I thought we might blow the roof off! Bye-Bye I say to Monsieur le Comte. I am now sorry I invited him and his wife to lunch. Almost ready for the festivities, but Madeleine has still not arrived. Maybe just as well? Things happen for a reason and if something has happened to her, there is nothing I can do. Maybe it would be a blessing not to take on all that responsibility. Didn't sleep well last night, but up and atem and moving forward!"

Punkin feel asleep in exhaustion after the *soiree*. She and Jean had a couple of moments alone away from his mother, and smooched like teenagers in a dark corner. Damien sold most of his work, The Club was happy with the proceeds for the evening that went to charity, and all had congratulated her. She got up, took Maurice for a walk in the brisk air, and ate a late breakfast. She took her cell phone on the walk in case Madeleine called.

About noon, her cell did ring and it was Madeleine. She sounded odd, out of breath, and scared. The upshot of the conversation was that she had finally made the break with Marcel, but had injured herself doing it. She was running to the refuge of Punkin and *Avenue President Wilson.*

To pass the time waiting for her arrival, Punkin got out her ironing board and placed it in front of the living room windows looking on the Tower. She always did her ironing looking at the Tower. It was fascinating to watch the changes in light. She started on her damask napkins for the lunch. She was going to use all her good china, sterling silver and crystal with flowers in profusion. Even in the winter months, flowers were plentiful and cheap.

The big clock in the hall chimed 2pm and the doorbell rang. There was Madeleine, bedraggled, bandaged, and loaded down with suitcases, canvases, drawing pads and a paint box. Punkin hugged her. She could feel her frail body shaking.

"Marcel almost killed me. He is so *mechant*, so evil. Look at my hand. I burned it so badly trying to escape from him. I will tell you all about it later. I was so ashamed at what happened, I went back to my Aunt's for a while. Sorry I haven't called you. I had to make sure Marcel wasn't following me, and I didn't want to lead him here."

She said all this in 10 seconds. She looked like she was ready to collapse. Punkin needed to settle her down.

"You should have buzzed from downstairs, Maddie. I would have come to help you with all this stuff. We will never let Marcel set foot in here!"

She carried Madeleine's bags into the second bedroom, which also had a view of the Tower. There were fresh linens on the twin beds, and a vase of tiny white roses on her bedside table. She helped Madeleine unpack. Her whole 20 years of life were in those boxes and suitcases. Besides the art materials and her clothes, there were several small boxes appearing to hold letters and photos.

"What's in the boxes?"

Punkin was curious.

Madeleine opened a box which did contain photos that had turned a sepia color with age. There were packets of letter, beginning to yellow, too. She handed Punkin some of the photos. Flipping through them rather quickly, one struck her eye. It was of a young man in a military uniform with his arm around a petite woman with long blonde hair. She looked at all the photos but came back to this one. The young man looked somewhat familiar.

"Is this your mother?"

"Yes, her name was Rose."

"Is the man your uncle?"

"No, my mother only had one sister, the Aunt I have been living with. The man, I think, is my father."

Punkin looked more closely. He favored Jean Aumont, but that was ridiculous. Coincidences like that only happed in the movies. She was a bit enervated by the possibility.

"Do you know anything about your father? At our first protégé meeting, I think you said you knew nothing at all."

"I know only what my Aunt told me. My mother apparently met my father in Paris before he left on military service. I think he went to Algeria, and never knew about me."

If there had been a hole in the floor, Punkin would have dropped through it. Holy shit, if this indeed was Jean, what would that mean? She did not want to stir a pot with either Madeleine or Jean, but how could she be sure? She let these thoughts pass. She did not want Madeleine to see she was disturbed.

"Have you ever tried to find your father?"

"I wouldn't know where to look. If he was in Algeria, he was too far away. *Tante Celeste* had no other information. As you Americans say, that is water under *le pont*, the bridge. I have managed to do without a father for 20 years. I am used to it."

Madeleine said this is a resigned little voice. It made Punkin love her more.

To change the subject, she suggested that they go into the kitchen and see what else needed to be done for Thanksgiving. Madeleine was starved, so Punkin made her a sandwich which she washed down with a big glass of milk. Maurice was so happy to see her, and jumped into her lap at the kitchen table.

The *maître d'hotel* from Thanksgiving restaurant was coming over at the end of the afternoon to go over final details for the lunch, which was in two days. There was nothing else to be done about the Jean/Madeleine conundrum now. Whatever happened, this was Madeleine's home, and nothing or no one was going to spoil that.

CHAPTER 18

La Fete de dinde

Turkey Day Arrives

Thanksgiving day dawned, and it started to rain. All the beautiful weather of the past few weeks disappeared. It had been replaced by gusts of wind, and strong rain pelting the windows. Just my luck, Punkin thought. No one will show up. It was hard to get people in Paris out in the rain. Taxis seemed to vanish, and who wanted to stand at a bus stop out in the weather?

Jackie, the *maître d'hotel*, was busy in the kitchen preparing the *aperitifs* and *hors d'oeuvres*. She heard that pleasing sound of champagne corks popping. Divine smells of roasting turkey and pumpkin pies was drifting out of the kitchen.

Punkin had just finished dressing. She had gotten her hair *coiffed*, and bought a new pants suit. It was light gray wool with a chinchilla collar and cuffs. The outfit accentuated her blond hair and cream complexion. Madeleine came into the bedroom and noticed a lovely *Hermes* scarf laying on the bedroom chair.

"May I wear this"?

"Of course, *Cherie*, that was my mother's. I think the color will look well on you."

She tied the scarf just right on Madeleine and looked closely at her face. She could see some resemblance to Jean and even more to Giselle. She pondered how she might address the situation. Jean would be one of her guests.

Madeleine was a little nervous.

"Tell me who is coming today. Will I know anyone?"

"Of course, you should know just about everyone. The Charlesons are coming and *Madame* Suzie, and Damien."

"Who else is coming? I think you said there were 14 *a table.*"

The other guests are our neighbors and our landlord Sebastian, his wife, and George Castellane. I invited Catherine *la gardienne,* too."

Punkin paused.

"And Monsieur Jean Aumont, a new friend of mine."

Madeleine noticed the way she said his name, he might be someone special.

"Is he your boyfriend?"

Punkin grinned, "Too early to tell."

Madeleine was counting on her fingers as Punkin ticked off the guest list.

"Punkin, that makes only 13 for lunch. The number 13 is unlucky."

"Oh Maddie, do not be superstitious. We had a last minute cancellation. Catherine's husband, Jerome, cannot make it."

Little Maurice trotted into the bedroom. He was dressed for the occasion, too. Punkin had found the cutest little doggie tux shirt. She knew he would not stay in it for long. It was unusually warm and humid this day.

"*Mon petit chien*, you will need to be on your best behavior today. You will have to stay in the kitchen, but can make a grand entrance after all the guests arrive."

The guests were invited for 1pm *precisement* for cocktails. They would sit down for lunch around 2:30. The Americans were always on time. The French always 15 minutes late. Their rationale was that they did not want to catch the hostess in her dressing gown.

Sure enough, at 1pm here came the Americans. It was the Charlesons and Suzie. Eleanor was carrying a big red box filled with chocolates. Suzie had a large bouquet of flowers. It was *bonne forme,* good manners, to bring a hostess gift.

Punkin kissed them all.

"Welcome my friends."

"*Bonjour et bonne fete de dinde,*" said Tom in his best French.

"Oh Tom, I think Happy Thanksgiving will suffice. I do not think the French even have a phrase for Thanksgiving. I guess 'holiday of the turkey' is close enough," said Eleanor rather impatiently.

Madeleine extended her hand to each of them.

Eleanor reached for her hand and said, "Hello Madeleine, I understand you are now *Madame* Lowery's houseguest."

Her tone was harsh. Madeleine was surprised. She thought *Madame* Eleanor liked her.

"I am so happy here. Punkin is like the big sister I never had."

The five some went into the living room. All were "gobsmacked" by the view.

"You didn't exaggerate that view. *Mon dieu, sacre bleu,*" said Suzie

" It is impressive, but we live so far away in the 7th. We had a devil of a time finding a taxi to come all this way over here," said Eleanor.

Tom grimaced. After 40 years of marriage, he was used to his wife acting like a pill.

Punkin called Jackie with a bell to bring in the champagne and nibbles. He entered carrying a large silver tray with flutes of champagne, glasses of orange juice and mineral water. The little *canapes* that she had bought at *Hediard* looked dainty and expensive.

"You have a *maître d'hotel*, how chic is that," said Suzie just loud enough to get Eleanor's attention.

Punkin said, "Who wants champagne? I have OJ and water, too."

"Never too early for champers," said Tom

"Since I am watching my figure, I will just take mineral water to start," said Eleanor

"What a waste of good champagne, Eleanor. I will join Tom," said Suzie

The three took their drinks as Jackie placed the *canapes* on the coffee table.

"Your dining table looks wonderful," said Eleanor.

At last, a compliment!

The table was gleaming. It was set in front of the large French doors in the dining area which lead onto the terrace. Punkin wanted to have the doors open today but with the *deluge*, that was impossible. The rain continued to come down hard.

"Do we know the other guests?" Eleanor inquired

"You have not meet my neighbors in the building or my landlord, who is a real Count. And, of course, I told you that I had invited my *gardienne*, Catherine."

Punkin just had to zing Eleanor about the "help" sitting at table.

"Your landlord is a Count? That is one thing which makes France so unique. Still so many royals around, although most resting on past glories," said Tom

"Are there any other Club members coming? Tom continued

"Yes, you know Jean Aumont."

"Ah yes, quite a nice fellow. Eleanor and I were pleased he wanted to join the protégé program."

Tom helped himself to another glass of champagne.

"Damien Hunter will be here, too. It might take him a little longer as he has to come all the way from *Montmartre*."

"Oh, dandy. We bought one of his pieces at the *vernissage*," added Tom

"And I thought he was very attractive," said Suzie.

They had just finished speaking when all of a sudden the French doors blew open, accompanied by a loud clap of thunder. Punkin ran quickly to close them before the table was drenched. The weather was spooking her.

"I hope this weather is not a bad omen. It was so pleasant the last couple of weeks."

She said this with a nervous laugh. Was anyone else coming?

At 1:30pm the doorbell rang and in came the French. First were the widows, Adele and Estelle, followed by dear George Castellane and *la gardienne*. Just as she was closing the door, she heard the elevator and there was Sebastian and his wife Michelle. Jean and a very wet Damien brought up the rear.

Only Michelle Richmond seemed on edge. She kept eyeing Punkin and then looking at Sebastian. He seemed ill at ease. Thankfully Punkin did not think anyone noticed their furtive glances. Jean kept smiling at Punkin, which all did notice. He motioned her to join him in the *foyer* for a moment. Once they were away from the crowd, he kissed her softly.

When something feels right, life moves along smoothly. In the weeks leading up to the holiday, Jean and Punkin had seen each other regularly and had that fabulous weekend in Normandy. They were taking weekly rides in the *Bois* and having intimate dinners at some of Paris' best *boites*. He was teaching her about wines, which she thought was a great hobby. America had good wines, but France had the best vintages in her opinion. He schooled her on the best years to buy. She learned that good wine was an investment. Wine makers based most of their children's inheritance on the quality of their personal cellars. Many of these wines dated back to the 1700's, were still drinkable, and worth a fortune.

She was delighted to learn that Jean loved to dance. He was quite graceful on the floor. He even knew how to tango. There was a famed tango school on the *Champs Elysees*. They planned to take lessons together. Punkin had a philosophy about love making. If a man was a good kisser, and a good dancer, sex would be great. *Eh voila*, it appeared so with Jean.

"*Merci bien* for including me today. We French rarely have the opportunity to celebrate a traditional American holiday. I was thinking it might be wonderful if we could go to the chateau before Christmas. Would that please you?"

Jean was holding her close.

Would it please her? Zowie, she was thrilled to her toes. A visit to the chateau would help her make a better impression on Giselle. Maybe that would be the time to address the Madeleine/Jean issue?

At 2:30 with everyone well lubricated, she called the group to table. She seated Jean at her right, and Tom to her left, and then boy-girl-boy-girl. There were more women than men, which always seemed the case all over the world. Once seated, Jackie brought in the first course, which was white asparagus with *vinaigrette*. They were in season in November, and a real delicacy. They began to chat.

"Jean, Punkin tells us that your family has a chateau in *Bordeaux*," Tom said as Jackie served him a glass of white *Bordeaux* with the asparagus.

"*C'est vrai,* that is true. The Aumonts have been making wine in the region for 4 generations."

Punkin interrupted.

"And, Tom, the wine we will be drinking with the turkey is from the Aumont vineyards."

Estelle Fontaine said, "Jean, I know your mother. We were at school together. Perhaps she can come to Paris soon for a visit."

Everyone began to enjoy their first course in silence. It must have been 20 minutes before the hour or 20 minutes after the hour. Punkin started a new topic of conversation.

"What is everyone doing for Christmas?"

Damien, to help her re-energize the group said, "I am going back to Louisiana. We have turkey for Christmas, but we fry it."

Estelle Jonville looked shocked. "You fry it? We French *fry frites,* but I have never heard of frying a bird."

That got the group to giggling. Oh the French, so different from *les americains.*

Jackie was just about to bring in the main course of turkey, sweet potatoes, and green bean casserole when all heard a loud voice in the *entrée*. Jackie came running into the dining room, precariously balancing the turkey on its tray.

"*Madame,* some *mec* just pushed his way into the front door!"

CHAPTER 19

A Disturbing Tunnel Before the Light

Marcel, the pimp, ran into the room, soaking wet and eye blazing.

"*Qui est Punkin?*"

His face was contorted like a deranged monkey.

The group sat transfixed. No one moved a muscle. The French women's mouths all dropped open at the same time, as if a puppeteer was pulling the strings. The men tensed up and were ready to defend Punkin's honor.

She stood up, and faced Marcel down with a defiant stare. At 6 feet, she was much taller than this thug, and she was going to use it to her advantage. You do not mess with a girl from Texas. If she had her shotgun, she would have blown him away.

"I am *Mademoiselle* Lowery. What do you want?"

Marcel walked up to her and stood an inch from her face. He came up to her about chest level. She could smell brandy on his breath. He must have drunk a lot of it.

"So you are the bitch who is trying to reform my Madeleine," he shouted.

He was dripping all over the carpet and smelled like a wet dog.

Madeleine, sitting at the other end of the table, looked terrified. He pointed to her and said,

"Let's go."

He didn't wait for a reply, and walked up to her. He grabbed her by the hair and out of the chair.

Madeleine screamed.

"You excrement, let go of that child!"

Tom stood up from the table.

Marcel let go of Madeleine and made a beeline for Tom. He picked Tom up, lifting him over his head. Jean grabbed at Marcel, but it was too late. Tom went flying across the table, landing on a table leg, busting his head open. Food, glasses, silverware, china and the plump turkey on the platter all crashed to the floor. Tom's head was bleeding profusely, and Eleanor was trying to stop it with one of Punkin's best damask napkins. Jean and Damien immediately tussled Marcel to the floor. Punkin rushed into the bedroom to call the *SAMU,* ambulance service, and *les gendarmes,* the police.

The rest of this episode was a blur. The ambulance arrived and took Tom to the American Hospital, Eleanor sobbing at his side. The police arrived shortly after and handcuffed Marcel to take him down to the city jail near the *Hotel de Ville*. The other guests, even best pal, Suzie, beat a hasty retreat. Michelle pulled Sebastian out first with an "I told you so" look on her face. The widows were fanning themselves, and looked ready to faint. Only Jean and Madeleine stayed behind. It seemed Punkin's social career in Paris was at an end. A shaken Jackie started cleaning up the mess.

With nothing left to lose, she thought, it might be as good a time as any to broach the subject of Madeleine's parentage. Since the living and dining rooms were a shambles, the only place they could talk was Madeleine's bedroom. She sat the two of them down, one on each twin bed. Looking at them in close proximity, there was a resemblance.

"Dear Madeleine and *cher* Jean. You know you are special in my life," she began.

She felt the emotional exhaustion of the day welling up. It was hard for her to speak without crying. She took Madeleine's hand in hers and said,

"Darling girl, will you do something for me? Get out the box of photos you showed me the other day."

Madeleine thought this strange, but of course did what Punkin asked. She handed Punkin the box, which she opened and thumbed through the photos to find the one. Turning to Jean she said,

"I want to show you something."

She placed the photo in his hands. His one good eye seemed to have trouble focusing. He looked at the photo, then at Madeleine, and then at Punkin. He continued looking at the photo as if in a trance.

Madeleine looked very confused. Punkin put her arms around her.

"I do not know how things happen in life. Many things cannot be explained. It seems maybe *Monsieur* Aumont is your father," she said

Hearing this, Madeleine looked at the two of them in shock, and fainted. They put her on the bed and waited for her to recover. They talked briefly in quiet tones before she came to.

"This is unbelievable. Can Madeleine be Rose and my child? I told you about Rose, the love of my life," he said

He paused a moment as if remembering it all. Madeleine was coming to. She moved away from them like an animal trapped in a cage, but was listening.

"Rose was not from the same class as me, so *maman* would not consider my marrying her. I had no idea she was *enceinte* with Madeleine when I left."

Jean started crying.

Madeleine stood up and began to back out of the room.

"*Non, non, non*, I have no father, I have no father."

She kept repeating this like a mantra.

Punkin stopped her from leaving and held her in her arms. Madeleine's sobbing shook the two of them. The three sat back down together on one of the beds. Jean began his story of his life with Rose.

He was 18 when they met and she was 17. Jean would come to Paris on the weekends and liked to dance at a little café in *Pigalle*. They had a wonderful band. One night he noticed a lovely young girl with long blonde hair and azure eyes. Her lithe body was swaying to the music. He could not take his eyes off of her. Jean could tell by her dress that she was not a *bourgeoisie*, from the upper classes. He felt a real chemistry as if he had known her before.

He asked her to dance, and that evening they never left each other's side. Rose explained to him that she lived nearby and was a struggling photographer. Her family did not have enough money to send her to university. She hoped to make a living with her photos of Paris. For six months they spent every weekend together. Rose was brought up Catholic, like Jean, so when they finally made love, neither of them took it lightly.

He wanted to marry Rose. It was the first time in his life he had truly been in love. He took Rose to meet Giselle. The visit did not go well. Giselle thought Rose low class, ill-educated and not half good enough for her only son. She raged at Jean that she would never allow him to marry her. Jean was close to leaving for his military service in Algeria, and because he loved his mother more than life, he acquiesced at first. For three weeks he did not go to Paris or contact Rose.

He was never more miserable in his life. He finally made a "man decision". He realized he could not be happy without Rose. Defying his mother, he and Rose made plans for her to join him in Algeria where they would be married. After he left France, they corresponded constantly. Jean thought his life was looking up.

Three months later, Rose was set to arrive by boat from *Marseilles*. He checked out of his barracks and went to meet the ship, loaded with flowers and good intentions. As each of the passenger disembarked, he expectantly looked for his love. She was not on the boat. He frantically called her family home. Her father answered and said Rose could no longer see him. That was the only explanation. Over the next few months, Jean kept trying to no avail.

A year passed and the wound started to heal. He met an Algerian girl, daughter of the *consul general*, who reminded him a lot of Rose. They began a relationship which led to marriage, but it was not a happy one. After a few years, they divorced. They were never blessed with children. He injured his eye in a rifle accident, and learned he would never see again out of that eye. Feeling sorry for himself, he thought no woman would want him. For the next 15 years, Jean concentrated on his military career and just forgot about romance.

When he finished his story, both Punkin and Madeleine understood.

"*Papa,*" Madeleine said with a little squeak as she embraced her father.

This was such a private moment, Punkin left and closed the door. She had some thinking to do. Her whole social status and life in Paris were at stake. She had no clue what to do about it.

CHAPTER 20

Moitie, Moitie

Glass Half-Full/Half- Empty

Punkin felt like she had a big red A plastered across her chest like Hester Prine in Hawthorne's classic novel. It had been a week since the "incident". Not one of her friends had called. The apartment on *Avenue President Wilson* was quiet as a tomb. She and Madeleine had holed up. Jean had not even come by. There were no invitations to accept or decline.

Punkin was humiliated when she had to go to the city jail to press charges against Marcel. Thankfully, her testimony and that of Madeleine's guaranteed that Marcel would be locked up for a while. He had no money for bail. Although she had not heard from Jean, she was secretly thrilled that he was Madeleine's father.

Thanksgiving evening turned out to be very special for the three of them. They sat eating what was left of the lunch, and drinking fine Aumont *grand cru*. They talked through the night, and Jean promised he would talk to his mother to arrange a visit to the chateau for both of his girls. No one was expecting Giselle to accept her granddaughter right away, but they had to make a start.

A bigger problem loomed. After the altercation, Punkin's landlords, the Castellanes, wanted her out. The French disdain any form of confrontation. The fact that an actual criminal had been on the premises was unacceptable. Leading the charge to evict her was her former paramour Sebastian. Only their son, George, wanted Punkin and Madeleine to stay.

She always tried to see the glass half-full. A move to a cheaper and smaller place might be the best thing. She was running out of money fast. The rent on this 2 bed, 2 bath, 1500 square foot apartment was over $4,500 per month. She made some money from the rental of her Houston townhouse, but with no job, her inheritance was disappearing.

It was finally a glorious winter day after all the rain. The sky was a brilliant blue with not a cloud. It might be enjoyable if she, Madeleine and little Maurice "took the air" and went for a long walk. Maurice could use the exercise. He sensed the tension in the house. He was starting to pee on the hardwood floors, an aggressive action by a normally well behaved dog.

They decided to walk up *Avenue President Wilson* to *Place Victor Hugo* and then over to the walking trails on *Avenue Foch*. The 45-minute walk would work up an appetite. They could stop near the *Arc* for lunch at one of the cafes on *Avenue Grande Armee*.

The girls were sipping their morning café in the kitchen when Madeleine asked,

"Do you really think *Monsieur* Jean is my father? It seems so unreal."

"It seems so, but I agree it is hard to believe. You heard his story, and have you noticed there is a resemblance between the two of you?"

"No not really, but if he is my father, **WHY** haven't we heard from him?"

Punkin did not have an answer. She wanted to stay positive.

"Maybe he is making arrangements for us to visit the chateau. Would you like to visit *Bordeaux*, and meet your grand-mother?"

"I guess, but will she like me?"

Punkin gave her a kiss

"Anyone who wouldn't like you is crazy."

Maurice was nipping at their heels and ready to go. Bundling up, they were just about ready to leave when the phone rang. Punkin left them at the front door to answer it. It was Jean and he sounded strange.

"Punkin, *c'est Jean, ecoute,* this has been a shock. I am trying to get comfortable with the fact that I have a daughter."

His voice was strained and there were no pleasantries.

"Have you said anything to Giselle?"

"I just told her I wanted to bring you for a visit and that your protégé might come, too."

"So, you didn't say you have a daughter."

Punkin was disappointed. Jean might be a momma's boy. She continued,

"I am in a state about this, too, because I don't think your mother liked me very much at the *vernissage*. When she discovers that I introduced you to a daughter you never knew you had, my ass will be grass as we say in Texas."

That bit of humor broke the tension and Jean laughed.

"Oh, Punkin, you are always *si drole*, so funny, with those Texas expressions."

"I know my mother and it is best to address this situation *face a face* in the comfort of her own surroundings. You know Adele de la Fontaine is a good friend of hers, and she may have told *maman* about Thanksgiving," he continued.

"Uh oh. But on the brighter side, maybe Giselle will like Madeleine more than she likes me and see the family resemblance," said Punkin.

Because Punkin was on the phone so long, Madeleine and Marcel came into the bedroom. She placed the phone close to Madeleine's ear so she could hear the conversation. She cautioned Maurice to be quiet.

"Your mother might take Maddie under her wing and teach her to be a grand lady," Punkin said as Madeleine smiled.

"I have asked Madeleine if she wants to make this visit. She is an adult, and doesn't have to accept either of you."

Punkin looked at Madeleine as she said this. Her facial expressions were so much like her father's. She knew Madeleine was counting on her father to come through.

"*D'accord*, just confirm with me in a few days what you all want to do, and I will set it up. Just tell me which train you are going to take and I will pick you up."

"I miss you," he said with a great exhale of breath

Punkin hung up the phone.

"*J'ai peur*, I am so afraid that my grand-mother will hate me! I am not of this class and scared of making many *faux pas*," said Madeleine.

"Don't worry, if you feel the least bit anxious, we can return on the next train. Might be a good idea to be prepared for that, and book a return ticket in the afternoon. I take it you want to go?"

"Of course."

"Let's go for our walk, and forget about our problems. Are we all ready?"

Maurice barked as if on cue.

They had a good *promenade*. Exercise is always an excellent way to take the blues away. They stopped for lunch at a restaurant on Grande Armee. The girls had *moules/frites,* mussels with fries. Little Maurice had a veal bone, nicely supplied by the *patron* of the restaurant. They returned to the apartment in much better spirits.

CHAPTER 21

Napoleon to the Rescue

Paris, November 28, 2000

"Mon dieu- My life is a soap opera! Thanksgiving is OVER thank goodness, but what a debacle. I have never been so scared, and humiliated at the same time. And finding out that Maddie might be Jean's child? Incroyable. Some good did come out of bad. From that look Sebastian's wife gave me, I think that affair is over, and it wasn't messy. Break-ups are always so messy. Now I just have to figure a way to get my friends back. I know they are all thinking, even Suzie, what a big mistake I made in involving myself with Madeleine. But it is a new day, and I will persevere. I think one always needs to keep an abiding faith that things will eventually go right."

Punkin decided she was not going to be a victim. She was going to take the high road, and reach out to her friends. They might just be waiting to hear from her. She decided to send e-mails instead of calling. She knew she wrote better than she talked, after all the years of writing snappy advertising copy. She was still very embarrassed about the episode. Her first e-mail was to dear friend Suzie. She would be the easiest to forgive, Punkin hoped.

"Dear Suze, I told you I wanted an unforgettable Thanksgiving- HA! Sorry for dragging you and everyone else into this drama. You were the first to tell me not to get involved with this child, but too late now. Give me a call. *Je t'embrasse*, Punkin."

Punkin would tell Suzie about Jean and Madeleine but no one else until things were resolved. She had to talk to someone. If only Big P was here, she would know what to do. She missed her mother and the comfort of her warm arms.

She pushed send, and was on to her next e-mail. This one was more difficult to the Charlesons. Eleanor was the *doyenne* of the ex-pat community, and her forgiveness was important to Punkin's future in Paris.

"*Cheres amies*, I apologize for the horrific events on Thanksgiving. Tom was my hero and I will never forget it. Your friendship means the world to me. I shudder every time I think of Tom getting hurt that way. I went into your protégé program hoping I could help. I do believe Madeleine can be saved from herself and I am going to continue to try. I will call you soon, and hope you can forgive me. *Je vous embrasse*, Punkin."

Next up on the *mea culpa* list were her two widow neighbors. Since they did not have e-mail, she was going to invite them to tea at the *George V*, and spend a lot of money on champagne to loosen them up.

She knew Damien would forgive her, so no need to apologize there. She would call him and say sorry and shoot the breeze. But, then there was Sebastian. That was another story. He would side with his in-laws the Castellanes. She was kind of glad that this had happened. It gave her a good excuse, and frankly, it gave him one, too, to end it.

Before contacting Sebastian, she decided to talk to his brother-in-law George, also at the lunch, and great pals with Punkin. Since he lived right downstairs, she called to see if she could meet with him in his apartment at cocktail time. She went down about 6pm and he had just gotten home from his law office. He greeted her at the door with a large Scotch.

"You are in *le merde*, dear girl."

She was in deep doo-doo for sure. He handed her the glass, tinkling with ice, and the soothing brown liquid. Punkin kissed him hello and followed him into his living room.

Although their apartment building was early 20th century, George's apartment was all contemporary with cool cream walls and pale wood floors. He had completely bleached out the beautiful *parquet d'hongres*, dark wood floors. What a waste, she thought. Plus, his collection of artwork was positively disturbing.

"*Cher* George, you are my *avocat* as well as my friend. I know I am in over my head, and your parents want me out."

"They are pretty concerned. We have never had police in the building before. You know the same families have owned these apartments since before World War 1. All our neighbors are worried. In fact, my parents are even checking to see if you are living legally in this country. The French have a sad history I am ashamed to say, of denouncing their friends and neighbors. The most intolerable episodes were during the 2nd War."

"FUCK"

What a descriptive word that is, and fits so many occasions. George laughed as she has said it. He had never heard her curse before.

"As to you having to vacate immediately, the law is actually on your side."

"I have no idea what are you are talking about."

"Well, let me get us another drink and I will tell you all about it."

As George went into the kitchen to fix the drinks, Punkin began to think about denunciation, anger, and superficial appearances. Maybe the French were not the "cupcakes" she imagined.

George came back and began his interesting discourse.

"French law is fascinating. My country has been through monarchs and five Republics. However, most of our laws are still based on the *Napoleonic Code*."

"You mean that little guy who was always painted with his hand in his vest? I always wondered what he was hiding in there, maybe his lunch."

Punkin was trying to keep it light.

George did not really get the joke.

"Be that as it may, he was a great man and made many positive changes for France. One of the best things he did was to insure that *les citoyens* were protected during our harsh winters."

"What's your point?"

This history lesson didn't seem to be going anywhere.

"My point is that there is still a law on the books called *loi d'hiver*. It is translated into English as law of winter. It says that no one can be thrown out of their lodgings in the winter months which are October to April. No constable or landlord can put a renter out during these months of the year, even if they do not pay the rent. My parents cannot make you leave now. You have five months to figure out what you want to do."

Punkin kissed him.

"Wow, that is a break, but you know France. It is all about social interactions and doing things the proper way. I would like to re-establish my relationship with your parents and all the neighbors. I do not want them to think I am the proverbial ugly American."

"I am happy you feel that way, but I have one question. Is your *carte de sejour*, resident card, in order?"

"Thankfully yes, and it was a pain to get. The French Consulate in Houston helped me and then when I got here, I went to the *Prefecture de Police* to register. I have to renew my *carte* every year."

She didn't tell him all the details of sitting in an airless room at the *Prefecture* with hundreds of others just wanting to "breathe free" in France.

"Good to hear. Now all you have to do is talk to Sebastian since he was in charge of renting you the apartment."

Punkin did not want to talk to Sebastian. She was happy George knew nothing about their affair.

"*D'accord*, I will take care of it."

"On another disagreeable subject, have you looked at your bank statement lately? I am glad to handle your bills, but you are getting a little low on cash. Do you have any additional assets?"

She took a deep swig of her Scotch.

"Unfortunately no, since I do not have a job here. I made myself a promise that I would only live in Paris as long as my money held out. But I can't leave now! You have no idea what else is going on in my life!"

George was surprised by her vehement response.

"I respect your privacy. I will say as your attorney and financial advisor, you should start looking for a cheaper place to live *toute de suite*."

They continued talking for about an hour. Punkin got home, a little inebriated, and began dinner for herself and Madeleine. Tomorrow she would take the widows to tea, hang the cost. She was waiting for Suzie and the Charlesons to reply to her e-mails. And, then there was Sebastian to deal with.

CHAPTER 22

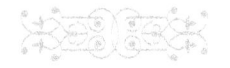

Showdown

The days were growing short. It got dark now at 4pm which was very depressing. The darkness mixed with the wind and cold left Punkin feeling sad. George was right. She was going to have to face down Sebastian, and look for a cheaper place.

The tea with the widows had gone well. They had always liked Punkin, and she did indeed fill them with champagne and good food. The afternoon started off a little rocky but then the widows were once again eating out of her hand. One down and several more to go. There was still no word from the Charlesons or even Suzie.

She called Sebastian and was very business- like on the phone. They settled on their normal meeting time of 5pm, but there would be no sex romp this afternoon. She made sure that Madeleine had something else to do, and she asked her to take Maurice with her. She needed total peace and quiet in the apartment for the showdown with Sebastian.

He arrived promptly at 5, and she could tell his attitude towards her had changed, too. It was like he was looking at her through different glasses. There was an awkward moment at the door when they would usually kiss. They didn't even touch each other, and went into the living room.

"Would you like something to drink?"

Punkin was being polite. The French always offer *quelques choses* to their guests.

"*Un café, s'il vous plait.* I can't stay long. Michelle is expecting me home."

He said this *sans* emotion. He could not look Punkin in the eye.

"I guess we should get to the point. I am fully aware that your in-laws want me out. I am sorry for that because I love this apartment. I always feel like a princess here."

"Yes, they are very upset about the Thanksgiving incident. We have never had any violence in the building There was also surprised you now have a roommate."

Man, word travels fast. I guess Sebastian had squealed to them about Madeleine. He was a bastard.

"My family and I have a social standing to maintain in Paris. It does not look well for us to have a *locataire* who invites convicts to the apartment."

Why had Punkin never realized what an asshole he was before? To call Marcel a convict was a bit of a stretch. Granted he was a pimp, but she had no responsibility for that, nor for his entering her apartment uninvited. She thought her former lover's attitude unyielding and narrow minded.

"It will take some time for me to find another apartment. George informs me I really do not have to leave until winter is over. That gives me months."

He looked at her in the coldest way.

"I suggest you move as soon as possible. It is true we have no authority to throw you out in the winter, but my on-laws are very powerful people. They can make your life pretty miserable if you delay too long. I am sure you do not want me telling them about Madeleine's past".

What a dick! Was that a threat? Punkin saw no reason to continue the conversation.

"I will see what I can do, but never threaten me. If you will excuse me, I have an appointment," she said in a curt manner

Her anger softened Sebastian, and he looked deeply into her eyes. He reached to touch her, but she wasn't having it. Maybe he felt guilty. She wasn't going to give him the satisfaction of thinking she forgave him. She put out her hand.

"Take care of yourself", she said
The relationship was over.
She ushered him to the door, closed it behind him and started to cry. Her life in Paris was not turning out as she had dreamed it. Had she been a gigantic fool?

CHAPTER 23

The Girls Visit Bordeaux

Bordeaux is an easy train ride from Paris on the TGV. Two hours, 30 and you are there. The center of the town is a little *triste*, sad, as the French say. It is situated on the *Garonne* River and its port, like that of *Marseille*, attracts an unsavory element. The ugly German concrete bunkers, now covered in graffiti, are still in place. The countryside around the town is where the region excels.

For centuries, the great wine conglomerates like *Lafitte* and *Chateau Margaux* have cultivated their grapes to make the best wines in the world. These families have large tracts of land and large manor houses dating to the 16th and 17th centuries. The Aumont family was no exception. Their chateau was situated near the small town of *Pauillac*, in the "second growth' area.

Jean was at the train station to pick them up. It was a 20- minute drive to the Aumont property. No one said much on the drive, so it was not clear to Punkin if he had said anything to his mother. She understood that he was going to tell his mother only that Madeleine was her protégé. All Punkin said to Jean on the ride was that they had booked a return train for later in the day.

They entered the magnificent iron gates of the estate and continued down a long gravel driveway. On either side of the road were rows and rows of vines. Most of the area was devoid of trees, unlike the other lush agricultural areas of France. The only vegetation in the *Bordeaux* Region was these vine plants, delineated by rose bushes at the end of each row. The roses were to keep the bugs off the precious *raisins*, the rationale being that the bugs would eat the roses and leave the grapes. This being early December, all the vines were bare. There was a sharp north wind which gave Punkin a sense of foreboding.

The Aumont "castle" had been built in the early 17th century during the reign of *Louis XIII*. It had a mansard roof of slate, thick 14-foot stone walls and a turret or two. Jean's mother was standing on the sweeping front steps of the *chateau* to greet them. She was dressed in "French country casual". She wore a cashmere sweater, plaid wool skirt, and an *Hermes* scarf. Her shoes were sturdy oxfords but of a fine quality, probably made by *Hermes*, too. The one time Punkin had seen her at the *vernissage*, she could not read her. Today was no different. Her lovely 80-year old face was a blank.

Jean helped the girls out of the car, and the three of them took a collective deep breath. They ascended the many steps up to the entrance and its sweeping terrace. Giselle extended her hand to Punkin.

"Bonjour Mademoiselle"

There were no kisses exchanged, and Giselle looked strangely at Madeleine.

"Oh, I see you have brought a friend."

Ok, this was not going to be easy. Jean had apparently said *rien*, nothing, to his mother in explanation of Madeleine. Just like a man to avoid the issue. Punkin had to make the introduction.

"*Madame*, I would like you to meet my protégé Madeleine Junot, a talented young artist."

Madeleine shyly took her grand-mother's hand as she studied her face. Punkin had made sure that Madeleine was dressed impeccably for this first meeting. She had dressed her in a fur jacket, and given her Big P's *Hermes* scarf to wear again. Since the girls had the same show size, Madeleine was wearing Punkin's *Roger Vivier* leather pumps. Giselle would be sure to notice all. *Haute gamme* women sized up other French women by the quality of their shoes, scarves and handbags.

Jean kissed his mother and gave her a warm embrace. The group entered the reception hall, and Punkin was struck by the richness of it all. A large staircase, seemingly carved out of one immense block of oak, lead up to the first floor. Along the walls of the staircase were portraits of the Aumont ancestors. Giselle had passed these portraits hundreds of times. If she would pay attention, she would detect some resemblance in Madeleine to this distinguished lineage.

The ceiling of the reception hall must have been 30 feet high. It was hung with huge crystal chandeliers that sparkled. Their appendages, like cut diamonds, made a tinkling sound in the light air of the hall. In the middle of the hall was a huge *Louis XIV commode.* In the center of this large cabinet was an impressive *Sevres* china vase filled with white flowers. The flowers gave the massive space a sweet, but cloying smell.

"Why don't we go into the *salon*?"

Jean said as he motioned the girls straight ahead.

Punkin needed a word alone with Jean. Her only excuse was to ask to use the powder room after their long journey.

"May I freshen up a bit?"

"Oh where are my manners? *Le toilette invite* is at the top of the stairs. Jean can show you," Giselle said

Punkin did not want to leave Madeleine alone with Jean's mother. However, she needed to find out what Jean had said about their visit. Jean and Punkin went up the stairs. When they were out of ear-shot, she asked,

"I guess by your mother's greeting, you have said nothing about Madeleine."

This was the first time in their relationship that she was actually miffed at him. Before the incident they had enjoyed many delightful, stress- free evenings. Jean was a much better lover than Sebastian and his "equipment" was larger, making Punkin a happy girl.

"I thought it would be better to see how things go."

What a cop-out. Punkin told Jean is her frankest tone that she really didn't see the benefit of prolonging the charade. They were only upstairs five minutes, but Punkin had made her point. They joined Madeleine and Giselle in the living room.

The *salon*, off the reception hall, was the main living space of the house. Deep cushioned velvet sofas in a rich royal blue were placed around the room. The room must have been 40 feet long. On the walls were rich tapestries Many side tables held precious porcelain *bibelots* and Oriental lamps.

Plush Persian carpets covered the hardwood floors. At the end of the room were a set of commanding French doors that lead to a stone terrace which overlooked the vineyards.

"Would you like tea or wine?" Giselle asked

Since it was a little too early for wine, they opted for the tea. Giselle pulled a big brocade cord next to the fireplace. The fireplace, made of slate, was enormous. Punkin could have stood upright in it.

In 30 seconds a butler arrived with the tea in opulent silver pots and more of the *Sevres* china for the cups and saucers. They began to converse with Giselle, who had all kinds of questions. She turned to Madeleine sitting on her right and said,

"So Madeleine, *vous etes de Paris*?"

Jean's mother was sizing her up. She wanted to see if this young girl was born in the capital or in the hinterlands.

"*Oui*, I was born in Paris near *Place Clichy.*"

Madeleine said with a pleasing smile, looking directly into the eyes of her grand-mother.

Giselle did not let on that she thought *Place Clichy* was one of the lowest and most common areas of Paris. It was the quarter of beggars, prostitutes and homeless in her opinion.

"And you are *Mademoiselle* Lowery's protégé? What does that mean exactly?"

Punkin jumped in to explain.

"*Madame* Aumont, Jean and I are involved in an American Club program which helps young girls enter the business world. I am sponsoring Madeleine in her artistic endeavors, and I am pleased to say she is doing very well."

Jean picked up the ball.

"*Mamie*, I told you about the protégé program. I am sponsoring another of the young girls myself. You know Eleanor and Tom Charleson. The program was their idea."

Good save, Punkin thought. Jean was redeeming himself a little.

Giselle seemed to find all these very strange. They continued their conversation with pleasantries about life in Paris, the wine making business, the weather, whatever. Giselle kept looking at Madeleine. She watched how she held her cup and saucer, gauged the correctness of her French, and how she interacted socially with the group. She finally said,

"I know the weather is a little brisk today, but would the two of you like to tour the grounds? *Loic,* our director of *viticulture,* would be happy to show you around."

Punkin knew this meant Giselle wanted time alone with Jean.

Loic was summoned by the same bell cord. He was an imposing figure, short but muscular, dressed in the green and beige checked jacket of the *vignerons* of *Bordeaux*. Khaki pants and heavy rubber boots completed his *ensemble*. He took the girls out through the French doors and into the vineyards. When they had left Giselle turned to Jean.

"*Mon fils, je ne comprends pas.* I do not understand why these two women are visiting. Why did you bring this horrible American and that *gauche enfante* here?"

"Mother, please sit down. I have something quite miraculous to tell you."

Jean told his mother in detail about Madeleine's birth, that he was sure she was his and Rose's child. He told her Punkin had discovered the secret from some photos that Madeleine had when she moved in to share the apartment.

He reminded his mother of his love for Rose and her implacable attitude in not letting them marry those many years ago.

"*Maman,* I think I deserve a little happiness, as does my daughter. I intend to raise her as an Aumont. I suggest you come to terms with it."

Giselle was pale, and looked all of her 80 years, but was not giving an inch.

"Jean, you are my only child, and heir to a vast fortune. I love you with my heart, but I do not know at this moment if I can ever accept this child. And WHY is this horrible Lowery woman insinuating herself in our affairs? All of this is none of her business! I will not acknowledge this young girl today, and certainly do not approve of your relationship with *Mademoiselle* Lowery."

She saw *Loic* through the French doors, bringing the girls back from the vineyards.

"*Zoot*, here they come."

Upon entering the living room, both Punkin and Madeleine looked for a sign that Jean had told his mother the news. Sadly, they realized from his expression that whatever had been said was not positive.

Punkin had made a good decision to book an early train home. It gave them the excuse to leave almost immediately.

"*Merci pour un tres agreeable apres-midi,*" Madeleine said as she tried to give Giselle a kiss. She stepped back and just touched Madeleine's arm.

Jean looked at both of the girls with a crest-fallen expression.

Punkin grudgingly thanked her as well, and they were off. Giselle ushered them to the door without saying a word about a second visit. The ride back to the train station was another quiet one.

CHAPTER 24

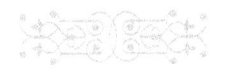

The Perils of Punkin Continue

Paris, December 5, 2000

"Well, THAT is over! I am so happy I booked that earlier train. Jean was a kind of a pill on the ride back to the station. I pray he is not a snob like my other boyfriend. I know this is a lot for him to deal with, and that mother of his. She still holds the apron strings for sure. And she just cannot abide me! I guess no matter how much I want to assimilate into the French way of life, I will always be in their eyes an 'Americaine', which is not a good thing."

They were both exhausted from the visit, both emotionally and physically. They made a light supper and then went to bed. Punkin was quite put out with Jean. She tossed and turned all night. There were so many things to resolve. She had gotten a terse *letter recommande*, registered letter from the Charlesons by the post. It said that they wanted nothing more to do with her, and enclosed a copy of Tom's medical bills for her to pay! This would be another predicament George would have to get her out of. She believed the letter was generated more by Eleanor than Tom. The two women just didn't see eye to eye on anything. The biggest peril facing Punkin were where she and Madeleine were going to live. She was ready to get out of this once dream apartment.

As often happens, the morning brought more hope than the middle of the night. She woke early and heard the happy sounds of Madeleine and Maurice puttering in the kitchen. Madeleine had been talking to Maurice like she did. She called to Punkin to say she was taking Maurice out for his walk. She could linger a little longer in bed. Before she could drift back to sleep the phone rang. It was Suzie inviting her to lunch. Thankfully, one of her friends was responding in a positive way. They planned to meet at the Hotel *Raphael*, one of her favorites. It had an *intime* bar where one could get a sandwich, albeit at a large price. The bar would not be crowded at noon and would be a good place to talk.

Madeleine and Maurice came back with pink and shiny faces from their walk in the cold. Punkin told her she was going to lunch with Suzie. Madeleine was going to her art lessons with Damien and was taking Maurice to meet little *Choo Choo*. At 12 noon they all headed out into the world.

Punkin arrived at the hotel before Suzie. She knew the bartender, *Jean Louis*, and ordered her standard *kir*, white wine and cassis. The hotel retained all of the old world charm she loved in France. It had been owned by the same French family for over 100 years. Many of the historic hotels in Paris had been morphed into garish, mirrored monstrosities by their Middle Eastern owners.

The bar was warm and welcoming, with red velvet couches and a huge oak bar. The room looked like a turn-of-the-century library. Suzie arrived in about 15 minutes in a bright mood.

"Hello *mon ami*."

Punkin hugged Suzie hard.

"Hello *ma chere*, don't squeeze the life out of me."

"Are you still up to your ass in alligators?"

Suzie added as she settled into the cushy sofa.

"What do you mean?"

Of course Punkin already knew the answer.

"I have talked to Eleanor and Tom. They are hot. You have put your foot in that. I think Tom is still a big fan, but Eleanor. She is ready to ban you from the ex-pat community."

Punkin raised herself on the couch and looked directly at Suzie.

"You don't know this part. I got a registered letter form them asking me to pay Tom's medical bills from the altercation with Marcel."

"You are kidding! That is insane. They are such hypocrites. They started the protégé program and it is because of them you met Madeleine."

"The only thing to be happy about is that Marcel is still behind bars as far as I know," said Punkin. hoping that was true.

She paused and then said,

"But there is now a bigger problem".

"What else is going on in your truly bizarre life?"

Suzie ordered her *kir* and sat back to listen.

"Hold on to your hat. After Maddie moved in, I found a photo of her mother with a man who bore a striking resemblance to Jean."

Suzie moved in closer to Punkin on the couch. She was almost on top of her.

"Well?"

It seems that Jean Aumont is Madeleine Junot's father."

"Get out!"

Suzie almost fell off the couch.

"It seems he never knew about her, because Giselle broke Jean and Madeleine's mother, Rose, up. Then Jean went to Algeria for his military service, and as you know was gone for 20 years."

Suzie had gulped down her drink and the girls ordered a bottle of wine.

"To make things worse, Madeleine and I went down to *Bordeaux* to see Giselle, hoping to come to terms with the situation."

"But that woman hates you," Suzie said

Punkin looked at her best friend in an annoyed way.

"Well, thank you Suzie, but Jean thought it might be a good idea, and I did too. Madeleine does look so much like her grandmother when they are side by side. We just got back yesterday."

"Don't leave me on 'tender hooks' as Scarlett would say. What happened?

"It went very badly. At the 11th hour, Jean caved and would not stand up to his mother. He told us on the ride back to the train station that his mother was having none of me or Maddie. He is sad about it, but it seems his mother is still ruling the roost."

"Leave it to an M-A-N to screw things up,"

Suzie was downing the wine pretty fast. Maybe she was thinking about her bastard husband in Georgia. They ordered their club sandwiches.

"I was dreaming of having a future with Jean. Then, when we found out that Maddie was his daughter, I might have a 'ready-made' family. But now, Giselle is holding all the cards and I feel totally powerless."

"Honey, your life is a melodrama." Punkin continued.

"One more goody on the 'shit' parade of my life. The Castellanes are demanding I move out. They were appalled about the Thanksgiving lunch. They said I had let a criminal into the building."

She took a big sip of the wine and finished,

"And I am shit out of money."

She had finally said that out loud. It kind of gave her a rush of self-confidence. She had nothing to lose. She would have to become an adult at age 50, and own up to her mistakes. There was no rich daddy to bail her out. It didn't feel bad. She was kind of calm about it.

"Having to move out is no biggie. I can certainly help the three of you (not forgetting Maurice) find a place to live. Y'all can always bunk in with us for a couple of weeks. My apartment, as you know, is huge and the kids would love having a dog around."

If they had not been in a public place, Punkin would have kissed her on the lips.

"You are the best, darling girl. That offer gives us something to fall back on. I probably will also have to get a job. George might be able to help me with that."

"See, things are not as bad as you think."

"What should I do about Tom and Eleanor?"

"Just sit it out for a while. Paris has a short memory, and quickly goes on to another *scandale*."

"At least I am through with Sebastian. We met at my apartment and he was so mean. He is a henchman lap dog for his in-laws, and a big snob to boot. WHY did I ever want to be with him?"

"It served your purposes for a while so do not beat yourself up."

They finished their two enormous club sandwiches and the bottle of wine. Punkin was not real hungry so she took ½ of the sandwich home for Maurice. Although the French do not do "people bags" they are always ready to accommodate *les chiens*.

CHAPTER 25

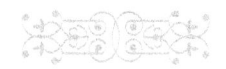

Die for Love?

Punkin didn't want to do it, but she had started selling some of her jewelry to build up a little "nest egg" for their move and the new apartment. Every time she went into the pawn shop, she felt ashamed. She hadn't been able to admit that fact to Suzie.

She started looking for an apartment immediately. She got a copy of the *Particulier a Particulier* or PAP as everyone called it. It was a huge weekly tabloid that weighed a ton. It listed all the apartments and homes for rent or sale in the whole country by owners. She was determined and remained positive. When one door closes, another is supposed to open. This could be a brand new start for her and Madeleine. She remembered the old line from Thorton Wilder's *Skin of Our Teeth*. Something like it was important to "eat the ice cream every day". The gist was one should enjoy every moment of life. She did have a lot to be thankful for, and she was in Paris. How bad could it be? She told Madeleine about the imminent move and she took it well.

To be economical, (something new for this Texas girl), she decided to start her search in parts of town that were really cheap. Most of Paris was pretty safe. The only areas you didn't want to live in were the 19th and 20th *arrondissements*. The center of town was OK. She found one possible in *Les Halles* around *Faubourg St. Denis*. It was one of the oldest quarters of Paris and had some beautiful *Haussmannian* buildings like the one she was living in now. They could get a large apartment for half the money she was paying now. However, in the last 20 years, the area had gotten a little "seedy".

The first apartment she looked at in *Les Halles* was near the *Centre Pompidou*. As she approached the building, she saw a "Lady of the Evening" slouching on the front steps. She was in an angora sweater, it being a very cold time of the year. The difference was that the sweater was completely cut out around her breasts exposing them. They were pendulous with nipples the size of 50-cent pieces. She was completely harmless, but yuk. Punkin did not even ring the bell for *la gardienne* to show her the apartment.

She spent the next couple of days making calls and visits. Coincidentally, she found an apartment on *Place Clichy*, where Rose had grown up. This area was gentrifying and was full of young artists. Maddie might like that. The rent was less than ½ of what she was paying in the 16th. She shuddered to think what Tom and Eleanor and even Suzie would say about her contemplating a move almost to *Montmartre*. She knew they would never visit.

It was December the 10th. Christmas was almost here. This day would become indelibly etched in her mind although she did not know it yet. It was a lovely, clear day. She and Jean were going for a ride. Nothing had changed with Giselle, but Punkin and her lover had made up. She was looking forward to the ride.

She met him at the *Polo* as usual and they started out on their ride. The horses were frisky and ready to go. All animals, including little Maurice, are invigorated by cold weather. Punkin hoped she and Jean could continue their discussion of the Madeleine issue. She would also tell him about the move. Maybe he could give her some good advice.

"*Cheri*, something has come up I didn't tell you about. Madeleine and I have to move out of *President Wilson* as soon as possible."

Jean looked surprised.

"*Pourquoi*, why is that?"

"It is all due to that horrible incident on Thanksgiving. Your countrymen detest drama. I guess it was too much for the *bourgeoise* Castellanes. They said in no uncertain terms, they want me gone."

"What are you going to do? Have you been looking for a place to live?"

Punkin, always the romantic, was fantasizing that maybe Jean would ask them to move in with him, although that was a little premature.

"I have been looking at lots of places but none really suits. We have been so spoiled living in that huge apartment. I will miss my view of the Tower."

"Just found someplace safe," he said

"I am not worried about that. Most parts of Paris are safe. But, my budget is much less than it was when I moved here. I want to find an unfurnished apartment this time so I can move all my furniture from the US and really make Paris home."

"That is a big step. I guess you plan to stay here for a long time?"

"Yes, you know I love Paris. How do you feel about that?"

"You should do whatever your heart tells you."

Punkin's heart sank with that non-committal response. She changed the subject.

"What is happening with your mother? I was kind of mad at you for leaving us hanging."

"You will be happy to know I have told her that I will accept Madeleine as my child. In a nutshell, I told her she could 'like it or lump it'."

Punkin laughed and patted his hand. He was learning some good American slang. They were riding in close proximity and the gentle up and down motion of the horses was like being in a rocking chair.

"I have a surprise for you. I told *maman* that I am bringing you girls back, plus Maurice, for *Noel* in *Bordeaux*."

Her boyfriend did have a spine. *Bravo!* Christmas in *Bordeaux*. She and Madeleine would wear Giselle down.

They started into a gallop. The change of the speed of the horses gave her a rush. She loved that sense of going from first gear into third. She was a pretty accomplished rider, but they were coming up to a low hedge which they would have to jump. She was a little afraid, and horses can always sense fear. Punkin's riding teacher had told her years ago that horses can either love you or kill you.

As they got up to the hedge, her horse reared, and Jean attempted to grab her reins. In doing so his horse reared up as well. Jean dropped Punkin's reins in an attempt to control his own horse. He was put off balance, and his horse took off in a straight run, veering into some trees to try to bump him off. Punkin calmed her horse and could see Jean moving at a high speed. After a minute, she lost sight of him.

She was agitated, but started slowly back on the trail. She did not want to spook her horse again. She finally caught up to Jean, and her heart stuck in her throat. He was lying on the ground, not moving. Somehow his foot must have gotten caught in his stirrup when he fell. His right leg looked mangled and was twisted at a 90- degree angle.

Punkin panicked. There were in the middle of the *Bois*, over 500 acres. Riders rarely passed each other on these trails, especially not in the middle of the week. She regained her composure and remembered her cell phone was in her riding jacket. She dialed the *SAMU*, paramedics. In her opinion the healthcare system in France was the best in the world, and she knew they would be there quickly. She gave them their location as best she could. Luckily they were near the *Chateau en L'ile* restaurant in the center of the *Bois*. The restaurant was well-known. The *SAMU* arrived in less than 10 minutes.

Jean had regained consciousness, but was totally disoriented. He didn't recognize Punkin. The paramedics loaded him into the ambulance and roared off, sirens blaring. They would take him to the nearby American Hospital. He would get immediate attention in their emergency room.

Punkin could not go with them. She had to walk the horses back to the *Polo*. That would take about 30 minutes, a lifetime. Jean was in danger. It brought back all her memories of Alex's suicide, and her mother's lingering death. Oddly, at that moment, she thought of some graffiti she had seen on a building wall in *St. Germain*. It said "*Mourir d'amour*", die for love. She didn't want Jean to die for love, but to live for it!

She finally arrived at the hospital. The news was not good. The doctors told her that Jean had fractured his leg in three places. The more serious problem was a concussion causing pressure on his brain and optic nerve. He might lose the sight in his one good eye. The doctors were keeping him in a coma to give his swollen brain time to recover.

Punkin had to call Madeleine and Giselle. Jean's mother would probably blame her for this accident. How would she ever win with this woman? She called Madeleine first because that was easier. She was at the apartment. Punkin did not tell her the full extent of his injuries. She did not want to alarm her while she was traveling to the hospital.

She then dialed Giselle's number. Her butler answered. It seemed like an eternity until she came on the phone. It was probably less than a minute.

"*Mademoiselle* Lowery, this is a surprise," she said in a cold way.

"*Madame*, Jean has been in a riding accident in the *Bois*. I was with him and called the *SAMU* right away. He is at the American Hospital."

There was silence on the line. Punkin could hear Giselle taking short breaths.

"How did this happen? My son is such a good rider."

"He was trying to help me. I lost control of my horse, and Jean reached for my reins. It threw him off balance, his horse bolted and carried him off. When I caught up with him, he was on the ground." As much as Punkin disliked Giselle, she didn't want to alarm this old woman, by telling her that Jean was hovering between life and death.

"This is all your fault! My son never should have gotten involved with you or that child. You have created all kinds of problems, and I will never accept either of you!"

Giselle was hissing into the phone like a reptile.

"*Bien entendu*, I hear you," was all Punkin could say.

She hung up the phone and knew Giselle would be on her way. It would take a good two hours or more, by car or train.

CHAPTER 26

TICK..TOCK...

A lapse of 60 minutes which embraces three thousand six-hundred Seconds of the time that flies- Edgar Allen Poe

Tick tock...tick tock went the hospital clock. Punkin was counting all those seconds and minutes. She was worn out. She had no energy for a confrontation with Giselle. Madeleine had arrived at the hospital, and took the news as well as could be expected. That poor girl could not get a break. The two sat in the waiting room holding on to each other.

"I have just found *papa*. I pray *le dieu* will not be cruel and take him away from me," Madeleine said with a tear in her eye.

She and Punkin decided they would put up with anything Giselle threw at them. They were prepared for accusations, and playing the blame game. Fate had a hand in Jean's accident just as fate had brought father and daughter together.

At 3pm, they saw from the hospital waiting room, Giselle's chauffeured car drive up to the entrance. Everyone in the waiting room had a good vantage point to see arrivals. This renowned hospital had as their patient's royalty, celebrities, and most of the ex-pat community. Giselle entered and came towards them. They could tell she had been crying. Surprisingly, she was cordial, but restrained. They all had something in common, their love for Jean.

"Is there any news?"

Giselle asked, her face choked with grief.

Punkin had no news. She told Giselle that the doctors had said this first night would be critical. The three women, spanning three generations in age, were at this point totally equal. They all loved Jean, and couldn't bear to lose him. Giselle was exhausted from her journey, so they went to the café for some strong French coffee. They returned to the waiting room watching the hands on the clock creep. At 6pm, the doctors came in.

"Who is next of kin?' One of the doctors asked. This did not sound good.

Giselle rose and said, "I am his mother."

The doctor shook her hand and said,

"The swelling in the brain is going down. However, we now have another problem. For some reason *Monsieur* Aumont's blood is turning acidic. We must give him a transfusion, and will need lots of blood. Can I check your blood for a match?"

"*Absoluement*", she said

Then Madeleine bravely stood up.

"*Monsieur le docteur*, I am his daughter. I would like to be tested, too."

Giselle looked horrified. How dare this girl insinuate herself. While Punkin waited in the café, both of the women's blood was tested. Jean's blood type was not the normal Type O but a rarer Type A. Giselle's didn't match, but Madeleine's did.

Maybe it was a blessing. A young girl would adapt better to the transfusion procedure more than an elderly one. It would take a good hour, and required Madeleine to stay overnight in the hospital.

Giselle came back to the café, and she and Punkin began to talk. Their emotions were at the breaking point.

"Well, *Mademoiselle*, I am happy that your protégé will finally do something worthwhile."

"*Chere Madame*, I know Jean told you about Madeleine. I would think at a time like this you might consider the circumstances if something happens to Jean."

Punkin said this as measured as she could, but there was steel in her veins.

"*Pardon?*"

Giselle knew full well what Punkin's implication was.

"Madeleine is your blood, whether you like it or not. I am sorry to speak to you so bluntly, but even if Jean recovers, he will want her in his life. And while I am being frank, I hope that life includes me."

Giselle stood up from the table as if to leave.

"You Americans always take what you want. I cannot stop you, but I promise I will not make things easy for either of you."

By 8pm the transfusion was over and the doctor came to tell them it had gone well. Because it was getting so late, and the two women could not overnight in the hospital, plans had to be made. The only answer was for Punkin to ask Giselle to come spend the night with her.

"*Madame,* it is so late and I am sure you are very tired. We will not know anything definite before morning. I suggest you come back with me to my apartment. I will make you as comfortable as possible."

"Don't you live in the same building as *Adele de la Fontaine*?"

"Yes, that's right"

"I would hate to impose on you. Adele and I are old friends, so I will call her and see if I can stay there."

Giselle was making the point that the last place she wanted to stay was with Punkin. As fate would also have it, Adele did not answer. Giselle was stuck with Punkin.

They took a cab and arrived in 15 minutes back at the apartment. Neither of them said one word. It was dark and very cold. Once they arrived, Punkin turned on all the lights, and lit a fire. She offered Giselle a brandy which she thankfully took. Little Maurice, who had been stuck in the kitchen all day, seemed to cheer up the old lady.

When she had finished her brandy, Punkin took her to Madeleine's room. She decided to try an experiment. She wondered if Giselle would be curious about the pictures of Rose and Jean in happier days.

"*Madame Giselle,* I am sure Madeleine would not mind if I showed you her photo box. There are many wonderful pictures of your son as a young man. These photos are the only mementos that

Madeleine has of her mother. I think it is so sad when a child loses her mother so young."

Punkin opened the desk drawer and got out the box. Giselle sat sphinx like on one of the beds, not knowing what to expect. She took the box and began looking at the photos. She smiled.

"I had forgotten how pretty Rose was. I only saw her that one time when they came to visit the *chateau*. I guess you know about that and how it went."

"Yes, he did tell me and Madeleine all about it. Since I have never been a mother, I can't imagine how I would have reacted. Maybe you thought you had good reasons for protecting your only child."

Punkin was turning on the sympathy, but she meant it. She didn't know what it was like to be a mother. Giselle, in turn, looked at her in a way that implied she might have misjudged Punkin.

Punkin sat at the desk in a chair. Giselle was still sitting on the bed. She seemed to be struggling to keep her eyes open, but her body and demeanor had relaxed somewhat.

"My whole life I have been so proud of our family heritage, perhaps too proud. You know Jean is so precious to me. I just wanted him to have a good marriage with a woman from a *bonne famille* like ours."

"And have lots of children," she added

"Punkin reached out to take her hand, which she did not pull away.

"That is completely understandable. But that is in the past. You now have the blessing of a grand-daughter if you will accept her. Can you not get some pleasure out of that? If you really look at Madeleine you will see a lot of Jean in her, and a resemblance to you."

Punkin could see that poor Giselle needed to go to bed. She got her a nightgown and robe and left her to go to sleep. She closed the door softly and went into the kitchen.

Punkin had to take Maurice out one more time. It was so cold outside, she hated to go out again. She was on edge and probably couldn't sleep anyway. She poured herself a small glass of scotch. She was not a brandy fan. She downed it in two gulps. It burned, but soothed her nerves almost instantly. She put on Maurice's leash and out they went. It had started to snow. What would tomorrow bring?

CHAPTER 27

Hope

The next morning there was much snow on the ground. Punkin had watched the flakes come down most of the night. Snow was so quiet, and much more soothing than rain, but she still could not sleep. She got up early and went down the hall to see about Giselle. She tapped on the door slightly, but got no reply. She opened it, and could see that Giselle was sleeping soundly. She looked very old and frail. For the first time, Punkin felt sympathy for her, rather than anger. Giselle suddenly woke up and saw Punkin staring at her.

"*Bonjour* Punkin"

It was the first time she had ever called her by her first name.

"I hope Madeleine will not mind, but I work up last night and started reading Rose's letters to her. It must have been heartbreaking to know she was going to die and not see her daughter grow up."

This woman did have a heart. Just as Giselle had misread Punkin, now the shoe was on the other foot. Punkin had not given Giselle any credit for being a fine person. She should have known that since Jean was her son. Apples do not fall very far from the tree.

"I do not think your grand-daughter would mind. These letters and photos might help you understand."

Punkin left Giselle to dress and went to her own bedroom to dress. She wanted to make sure they could get back to the hospital quickly. They would first check on Madeleine after the transfusion. Punkin had been praying all night that this morning she would hear some positive news about Jean.

She fixed them a quick breakfast and then they decided to ride the bus. Taxis were so hard to find at rush hour. The 82 bus, which went directly to the American Hospital, was right outside Punkin's door. They waited five minutes and got to the hospital in 20. They had no idea what to expect, but held on to each other.

The news was hopeful. Jean had improved. The swelling in his brain was almost gone, and he would not lose the sight in his good eye. The transfusion had been a success, and he was out of critical condition. He would have to stay in the ICU for a day or two. His fractured leg was not as serious as originally diagnosed. He could not see well out of his good eye, but that would improve the doctors said. They could go in one at a time to the ICU, but only for five minutes per visit.

They went to Madeleine's room where she was up and enjoying her breakfast. Giselle's attitude towards Madeleine was softening. She did not greet her grand-daughter effusively, but much friendlier with a smile on her face. Madeleine would be discharged as soon as she dressed. The three women would take turns going in to see Jean in ICU.

Giselle was first. She didn't say much when she came out of ICU but her eyes were red and puffy. The girls didn't pry because they were not close enough to her yet. They quietly helped her to a chair, outside ICU, and Punkin stayed with her while Madeleine went in to see her father.

She was surprised to see her father so alert, trying to sit up. When Jean heard Madeleine's voice, he grinned. He could only make out shapes of people and groped for her hand in the direction of her voice.

"*Ma chere fille*, the doctors told me you saved your *papa's* life."

"*Cher papa*, I will be here every day until you are well. *Grandemere* is being a lot nicer to me. Maybe we can be a family," she said as she hugged him every so gently.

"Wonderful! When did all this start?"

"She came home to stay with Punkin last night. She is still distant, but much better than when we visited in *Bordeaux*."

"Take it slow *mon enfante*. She is an old woman and set in her ways. She is not used to either of you."

She kissed him on the forehead.

"I will let Punkin come in to see you now. She has been waiting and is getting impatient."

Punkin had gotten Giselle a cup of coffee and she seemed calmer. Madeleine took over watching her as Punkin entered ICU.

Punkin tiptoed over to Jean's bed. He looked so small and weak. He had closed his eyes for the moment and she leaned down to give him a kiss on the lips.

"Punkin," he said in a whisper

"My love, I feel the accident was all my fault.".

She had not been able to help Alex or Jean.

Jean traced Punkin's face with his hands, and kissed her.

"Do not worry my little girl, nothing was your fault. Madeleine says that you and mother are getting along better."

"Slowly, but I am not expecting any miracles. I have asked her to stay with us until you get out of the hospital. She is sending for some clothes and personal items. We hope you will be out of the hospital before long."

"I have the thought of my three girls and a joyous Noel to help me get better fast."

He saw a glimmer of Punkin's long blonde hair as she lingered over his bed. Most things were still in shadow, and he prayed his sight would return to normal.

Punkin was sitting close to him on the bed, stroking his arm.

"I know you are getting tired, but I will say one last thing. I showed your mother the pictures of you and Rose. And then Giselle read some letters Rose had written to your little girl. I think she understands the whole situation much better now."

"Maybe this is the season of miracles," Jean said

Punkin could see Jean needed to sleep so she tip-toed out and rejoined Madeleine and Giselle in the waiting room. The three women had a short meeting with Jean's doctor. Although the prognosis was for a complete recovery, he told them that Jean would probably have to stay in the hospital at least 2 weeks.

The three women fell into a daily routine. They got up early, dressed, had breakfast together and then came to the hospital taking shifts to visit Jean. He was now in his own room which meant they could spend most of the day with him.

Living together in close proximity at *President Wilson* was a little tense, especially since Giselle was sharing Madeleine's room. As the days passed, it got better. Punkin would hear laughter coming from their room, always a good sign. Giselle and Madeleine started taking little Maurice on his walks. One evening, at bedtime, she walked by their room and saw them sleeping side by side. Their resemblance to each other was striking, both in facial features and expressions as they slept.

In about 10 days, the doctors were saying that Jean would be released for the Christmas holidays. Doctors didn't like to keep patients in a hospital over a holiday. Jean had made great improvement. His eyesight had returned to normal, and his leg was healing well. After the transfusion, there was no other indication of problems with his circulation or his blood.

Giselle and Punkin were bonding over their favorite subject- Jean. Giselle told her so much about his youth. She filled in a lots of blanks about his life before she knew him. They were all excited when they got the news that they could take Jean home, just in time for Christmas.

The doctors agreed to let him be transported by private car back to *Bordeaux*, but recommended Giselle hire an *infirmiere*, nurse-practitioner, to come to the chateau. Jean would need daily therapy to improve his walking. Everyone was anxious that something might go wrong, but it didn't.

CHAPTER 28

The Holidays Begin

Paris, December 23, 2000

"Almost Christmas, and our blessings abound. Giselle, Maddie and I have been shopping like mad for the holidays and Jean's return home. I think angels are still looking out for me. I was in the beauty shop yesterday, and the strangest thing happened which is still on my mind. A woman, seemingly homeless, but not badly dressed, came into the shop. She was asking for money, and everyone ignored her. It was raining like mad, and she had come in soaking wet, with no umbrella. She asked the shop owner if she could sit a while until the rain stopped and the owner said yes. I watched her, and she had such a quiet dignity. Maybe she was an angel come down to earth to check things out. The world has been in such a turmoil of late, I think angels are coming to see who is being 'worthy' and who isn't. I just felt such a strong urge to help her. She got up to leave, and I gave her my umbrella. I could tell by the expressions on the other client's faces, they thought I was weird, since I only had a hat and it was still pouring. I handed it to her, and she smiled. I felt I had been touched by an angel. I know, Punkin, you sound crazy, but it was true. I followed her out shortly after and she had disappeared as if into thin air."

December 24th, Christmas Eve: *La famille* Aumont were all excited. Today they were going to the hospital to take Jean home. Madeleine, Punkin and Giselle had gotten into the holiday spirit once they knew he would be OK. They did loads of Christmas shopping and bought tons of presents. All the gifts were wrapped in bright red with silver and gold ribbons. The three women all hid their presents from the others.

Punkin got Jean the biography of his hero, *Charles de Gaulle*, plus his favorite cologne from the men's store *Creed*. Madeleine got her father a soft cashmere scarf in navy blue to match his eye. For Giselle, they had picked the presents together. It was a splurge, but worth it. They bought a small *Lancel* bag in bright red leather.

She would think it too bold, but the girls were going to stir up the staid Aumont household. Punkin had discovered Giselle's favorite perfume was *Caleche* by *Hermes*, so they bought a bottle.

Punkin had a surprise gift for Madeleine. She would wait until they were all together *chez* Aumont to give it to her. Giselle must have been doing a lot of shopping, judging from the many packages surrounding her bed in Madeleine's room. She was happier now. One afternoon, Punkin found her humming a little tune, and gaily wrapping presents. When Punkin caught her, she hid the packages like a little kid, and giggled.

The morning of Christmas Eve, the Aumont chauffeur arrived at *President Wilson* to pick them up. They would continue on from there to the American Hospital to pick up Jean. The limousine was loaded down with packages, suitcases, a *buche de noel*, (the traditional Christmas log cake), bottles of champagne and gourmet goodies from *Fauchon*.

The trip to *Bordeaux* and then on to *Pauillac* takes around 2.5 hours if there is no traffic. Since it was Christmas Eve, it might take longer on the *auto route*. The nurse brought Jean to the hospital entrance and they helped him into the car, stacking pillows around him for the long ride, wrapping him in to some warm blankets. All three of them smothered him in kisses which started him laughing as if being tickled to death.

They all talked non-stop on the trip home. Little Maurice was riding in the front seat with the chauffeur and had a big red and green bow tie around his neck. The driver rolled the window down, and Maurice stuck his head out of the crack to feel the wind and brisk cold. Upon arrival, near sunset, the chateau looked spectacular. The gravel drive was lined with votive candles in paper bags, all the way to the front door. A large outdoor Christmas tree with colorful ornaments and lights was placed on the front steps. The inside was more festive than the outside. Entwined along the grand staircase were garlands of evergreens each tied with a red velvet bow. Another massive tree about 20 feet tall was positioned in the reception hall, ready for the colorful packages.

They would not make this first evening a long one. It was already dark when they got to the chateau. Jean was tired and needed to get in bed. But first, they would drink a little champagne and each open one present. Jean would be on the ground floor in the office that adjoined the living room. It would be too difficult for him to climb the stairs just yet. Giselle was putting Madeleine and Punkin down the hall from her on the first floor. (Note: the first floor in France is really the American second floor.)

In the living room/*salon* a roaring fire in the grandiose fireplace gave out a warming heat. Through the French doors, one could see the terrace trees lit with twinkle lights. It was a fairytale setting.

The four of them settled into the soft velvet sofas, and the butler brought in two big bottles of champagne, and some of the *hors d'oeuvres* bought at *Fauchon*. Because Giselle was the *matriarch*, she opened her present first. It was the bottle of *Caleche*. She sprayed some on, and thanked the girls. It was so thoughtful of them to know her favorite perfume. Then Jean opened his which was the cashmere scarf. Madeleine tied it in a jaunty knot around his throat.

Then it was Madeleine's turn. Punkin had a time all these weeks hiding this present from Maddie. She now took it out of her purse.

"*Ma chere,* on this Christmas day, I want to tell you how much joy you have brought into my life. That is why I want to give you this."

Madeleine was intrigued. She thought she had seen all the presents. As she opened the small satin box, her eyes filled with tears. Punkin had given Madeleine her most cherished possession, her mother's pearls. The two embraced.

"My mother always wanted me to pass these on to my daughter. And now, I am."

Punkin helped Madeleine put them on. They both looked at Jean and Giselle. Madeleine went over to her grand-mother and hugged her, and then Punkin hugged Jean. The joy in the room was palpable. There was still another surprise.

Under the tree in the reception hall, the chauffeur had placed a large rectangular box, wrapped in layers of tissue paper. The girls had wondered what it was because it was so large. Jean asked Giselle to ring for the butler to bring it in. Even she had no idea what it was.

All eyes were on the packet as the butler brought it into the room.

"Madeleine, I want you and your *grande-mere* to open this together," Jean said.

The butler placed the large box between them. They tore off the paper. They couldn't believe their eyes. In the box was the portrait of Madeleine that Damien had done. Jean had seen the portrait at the *vernissage*, and admired it. When he discovered that this lovely child was his daughter, he secretly arranged to buy it from Damien. He had done this just before the accident. Damien had guarded the secret well.

Giselle looked at the portrait and then at her grand-daughter. She finally recognized the resemblance to the Aumonts. Giselle promised all that the painting would hang on the stairway with the other ancestors.

Three of them had gotten their first presents, but what about Punkin? She had been so excited playing Santa Claus, she had forgotten about herself.

"And now for the *piece de resistance*. We have saved the best for last. Madeleine made all the arrangements, but the present was my idea," said Jean with a grin.

As if on cue, *Loic* opened the French doors and standing there was the most beautiful Palomino horse that Punkin had ever seen. The gentle mare had a beautiful saddle, (probably *Hermes*), and red ribbons plaited in her mane. Punkin squealed!

"We named her 'Chiquita Banana", father and daughter said at the same time.

There would be one other present for Punkin during this Christmas. A small red box was hiding under the tree.

Giselle raised her glass and said,

"I am an old woman. Old people get set in their ways. They often do not see the glories of life that are all around them. It took almost losing Jean to make me realize that family is the most important thing in life, no matter who they are, or how you find them."

This seemed to be an ideal start to the coming year. But, as in life, no one ever knows for sure. This family needed time. During this season of hope, at least, they were on their way. What the coming year had in store, *qui sait,* who knows? It was too early to tell.

End of Part One

PART TWO

*Madame Aumont,
nee Punkin*

CHAPTER 1

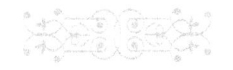

IS Paris Perfect?

Punkin, Jean and Madeleine returned from a wonderful holiday at the Aumont Chateau. After 2 weeks in the brisk country air, Jean was mobile and healthy again. Punkin encouraged him to start riding again as soon as possible. Plus, she loved their rides in the *Bois de* Boulogne, *La famille* Aumont had bonded over the holiday but the future was not clear. There was still the issue of whether Giselle would accept Madeleine as an Aumont, and accept Punkin as Jean's wife.

That little red box under the tree had contained a monster diamond engagement ring for Punkin. She hoped she would soon be Madame Aumont. Giselle, however, was not in the fold and an American daughter-in-law was not in her plans for Jean.

Giselle had hoped that Jean would marry one of those stick-thin French *bourgeoisie* girls who had nothing to say and were content to let their husbands and mothers-in-law dictate their every move. These women were trained from birth to expect their husbands to have mistresses, but to grin and bear it. At least they would have their husband's name, the wealth and the prestige. Their husbands were kind of like an ornament to be shown off like their designer clothes.

No date had been set for a wedding. Punkin and Madeleine had more pressing matters. They had to move from *Avenue President Wilson*, and quick. The Castellanes were adamant they leave the building at the first of the year. Jean had no room for them in his tiny *pied a terre* in Paris. He only used it occasionally and was spending more time in *Bordeaux* learning the family business. Giselle had gotten her wish that he would continue the tradition of producing the House of Aumont *grand cru*. He had a lot to learn, and *Loic*, the head *vigneron*, was teaching him all the steps from the harvest to the fermentation to bottle the family's renowned wine.

January was too harsh and cold to expect a good crop of *raisins* for the September harvest. The grapes would take months to bloom, but sweet Madeleine, finally in the loving arms of a family, was blossoming! Giselle was instructing her in the social graces, and Madeleine was a quick study. She had the looks and regal bearing. She only needed a push to be a true Aumont.

Punkin and Madeleine returned to *Avenue President Wilson* in uplifted spirits and began to pack. A family decision was made that the "girls" would live briefly in a furnished apartment until Jean could find a suitable place for the three of them. As luck, would have it, dear friend Suzie had found the perfect place near her apartment on *rue st peres* in the 6th *arrondissement*. It only had one bedroom, but they were happy to share. Punkin wanted to keep to a budget until she was sure she was going to be Madame Aumont.

Marcel, the pimp, had been locked up after the altercation on Thanksgiving. However, since no great crime had been committed, his sentence was projected to be a short one. He might get out as early as the spring. As least Punkin and Madeleine would be long gone from *President Wilson*, and Punkin felt assured that there would be no way he could find them.

Madeleine had finally told Punkin all the sordid details of her life with Marcel. It made Punkin mad enough to kill him. She would never tell Jean, because he would kill Marcel.

Punkin was constantly amazed how resilient Madeleine was. Her little girl had put that behind her, but Punkin feared the pain still lingered.

Valentine's Day was the scheduled date for their move to 9 *rue st peres*. Punkin was thrilled she would be through with the imperious Castellanes, but would miss their son George. They had so many good times together. At least she would continue to see him as he would remain her lawyer. She would also miss her *grandes dames* Adele de la Fontaine and Estelle Jonville on the second floor.

There was a new addition to the family. Madeleine loved little Maurice, and suggested to Punkin he needed a companion. Little Babette arrived. She was a terrier like Maurice, but only 6 months old. Maurice acted like the proud papa and immediately took to her.

Suitcases, doggie carriers, and art supplies were packed into the moving truck and *on y va*, away they went to their new home.

Moving day on February 14th was liberating and romantic. Jean brought the girls armfuls of roses, boxes of chocolates and of course, bottles of the Aumont red to help with the move. Moving from the staid, constricted 16th to the free and artistic 6th was exhilarating especially for Madeleine, who needed to be in a younger quarter of the City.

Their temporary apartment was on the 4th floor. *Rue st. peres* was right off of *Boulevard St. Germain*, just a short walk to *St. Germain des Pres, Les Deux Magots* and *Le Café de Flore*. The bell tower on the St. Thomas d'Aquin church chimed every hour and its "boom" reminded Punkin of the massive grandfather clock on *Wilson*. One could never forget what time it was in Paris as every clock on every building always showed *les temps precises*, the exact time.

The furnishings of the apartment were less elegant than *Wilson*. One could tell it was a hodge podge of hand me downs, but it was OK. With a little effort Punkin and Madeleine could make it home. Suzie arrived on moving day with her children and loads of food to stock the pantry. The Gilmores were unfortunately moving back to the U.S. quite soon. Suzie's divorce was not going well, and she needed to be back in Georgia to straighten it all out. Her son, Christopher, hated to leave, but daughter, Charlotte, was ready to get home to her friends.

What would Punkin do without her best friend in Paris? They had been through so much together in the last 18 months. Suzie had talked Punkin through her affair with Sebastian, and the horrible incident with Marcel on Thanksgiving. She had given Punkin some great advice for which she was grateful. She would miss Suzie and her free-wheeling spirit a lot.

She was hoping Suzie would come back for the wedding whenever that was. Jean had become very vague on that point. Punkin reasoned, of course, that it was Giselle hoping the marriage would never take place. Giselle seemed ready to claim Madeleine, but Punkin? Giselle was not convinced she would fit into the Aumont lifestyle, and frankly, Punkin was not either. The one thing she had no doubt about was her love for Jean.

Punkin had finally stopped trying to please Giselle. Jean, however, was still under his mother's spell. Not surprising behavoir since he was an only child and the apple of his mother's eye. Disturbingly, he and Punkin had started having arguments about the future. Their relationship was becoming a little strained. She had Madeleine, she thought she had the love of Jean, but would Paris be the perfect life for her? Reality was never better than dreams. Her anticipation of riding off in the sunset with her knight, and her white picket fence life were tarnishing a bit at the ages. As she usually did about anything in life that did not please her, she would think about it tomorrow.

CHAPTER 2

Door codes, Seagulls, and Things that go bump in the Night

Day to day living was beginning at 9 *rue st. peres*. Another set of door codes to remember. Paris was full of door codes. There were those of your own for the main door; the inter-door; your bank account; and the door codes of your friends. When the girls first moved in they kept punching in the doors codes for *President Wilson* or their credit card pin numbers. It was even worse at night for Punkin. After dark, it was hard to see the door code panel on the exterior, and she would always have to find her reading glasses in her purse just to get into her own building. Someone with a bad memory could not live in Paris

The neighbors were a mixed bag of artists, students and retirees. *St. peres* was a more modern building than *Wilson*, being Art Deco, not Haussmanian in style. The girls soon discovered that the walls were paper thin. Their next door neighbors, a young married couple, liked to make love early in the morning and the wife had the most delightful laugh coming through the walls. And, like clockwork, every morning at 4am, the little baby on the 2nd floor would start crying, waking up for its day. The consolation of *st. peres* was its proximity to the River. They could hear the seagulls every morning on the *Seine*. It reminded Punkin that Paris was indeed a port city with the mighty *Seine* running into the Atlantic Ocean.

After they had been there about a month, they were awakened at 1am by the sounds of Led Zeppelin booming from the apartment above. Looking out of their window, they could see strobe lights flickering like in a disco. Since there was a law in Paris that no loud noise was tolerated after 11pm, Punkin decided to call the police. She dialed the number of the *Prefecture* in the 6th and someone answered immediately. She explained the problem in her now prefect French and the policeman on duty said it would be taken care of.

Miraculously, 5 minutes later, no noise was coming from 9 *rue st. peres*. Punkin was amazed. She had not heard a police car, nor heard anyone enter the building. Maybe the *gendarmerie* had called *la gardienne*. Their new *gardienne*, Antoinette, was *tres charmante*, but was older than their *gardienne*, Catherine, on *President Wilson*. She was married with a grown son of about 18 who was making eyes at Madeleine as soon as they moved in. Punkin had tipped her generously when they had first arrived. That counted for a lot for future assistance.

One always gave *la gardienne* little tips for services like accepting deliveries, keeping keys while one was travelling, or just keeping a look out for the security of the building. In addition, at the first of the year, not Christmas, when Americans exchange gifts, it was good form to give the *gardienne* a *Meilleurs Voeux*, good wishes card for the start of the year, with money, wine, a plant or all three.

Gardiennes could be your best friend or your worst enemy. They were the biggest gossips in town, and could tell you with relish everything about your neighbors. Punkin and Madeleine were going to keep their heads down and not be fodder for any gossip. Jean had decided not to ever be present at the apartment at an "indecent" hour, and *jamais*, never, would he spend the night.

After the noise subsided, Punkin lay awake for a long time in her twin bed next to Madeleine listening to her breathing. She had spent so much of her existence alone; it was such a comfort to have life in the apartment and hear something else besides her own voice.

Tomorrow was Sunday, a big family day in Paris. Giselle was coming up from *Bordeaux* and they were gathering at *Le Pres Catalan* in the *Bois de Boulogne* for lunch. This elegant restaurant, in existence since the 1800's, had a lovely heated garden where one could dine amidst abundant flowers even in the dead of winter.

CHAPTER 3

Dejeuner Au Famille

Lunch with the Family

It was "Spring forward" Sunday, and everyone lost an hour of sleep. The inhabitants of 9 *rue st. peres* were in an irritable mood. The alarm, set in plenty of time for the girls to get into their finery, had not gone off. Punkin and Madeleine were struggling to wake up and meet their 1pm lunch deadline. From the 6th it would take longer to get to the *Bois de Boulogne* in the 16th, which was nearer their old apartment.

Giselle had been buying Madeleine some elegant clothes in addition to giving her lessons in comportment. Today, Madeleine would wear her new Chloe wool sheath in a soft violet that brought out both her ebony hair and blue eyes. Giselle had also bought her a violet colored cashmere coat, so *parfait* for spring. The finishing touch was Punkin's mother's pearls which Madeleine always wore, even with jeans.

Our girl Punkin never liked to be in a rush. Bleary-eyed, she peered into her closet to find something appropriate to wear. It had to be both elegant and conservative to suit her future mother-in-law. She still had to take Babette and Maurice out for their walk. The wind was strong this spring day. It woke one up, but also ruined any semblance of a nice hair do. Punkin thought she might wear a hat. That would please Giselle.

At 12:30 the girls got on the 63 bus to *La Muette*, and then took a taxi the rest of the way into the *Bois*. Punkin was a little miffed that Jean was not picking them up. Giselle was still calling the shots for her "little boy" and *maman* liked to have Jean all to herself.

When Punkin and Madeleine arrived at restaurant, the Aumonts were already seated at the best table in the garden. The Aumont name counted for something in Paris as well as *Bordeaux*. Jean rose to greet them with a big kiss. Madeleine embraced her grand-mother and Giselle rose half-way to kiss Punkin on both cheeks. *La famille* quickly ordered 4 *coupes de champagne*.

"*Bon dimanche*", Jean said as he raised his glass gazing at the three people he loved the most in the world.

"I think this might be a good day to talk about the wedding," Giselle smiled.

Punkin was surprised and pleased that Giselle was admitting there would be a wedding.

"I think that is a wonderful idea, but Jean and I have not even talked about a date. We still need to find a place for the three of us to live," said Punkin stoically.

"We, of course, will have to do the reception at the Chateau. The civil service can be at the town hall, and then I thought the church service could be in the Aumont family church in *St. Emilion*" said Giselle, totally ignoring what Punkin had just said.

Uh oh, thought Punkin. I am not even going to be able to plan my own wedding. She held her ground with Giselle.

"I was thinking since Jean and I have so many friends in Paris we would do the church ceremony here. I have become a member of the American Cathedral on George V. I love the Dean there, and have already mentioned to him the possibility of marrying us."

"You know, Punkin, Jean is Catholic and I would expect you to convert and take classes before your marriage", said Giselle.

Both Jean and Punkin looked perplexed. Jean was spiritual, but not very religious. Since there would not be any additional children to raise in the faith, he thought the idea ridiculous. Punkin agreed.

"With all due respect Giselle, I enjoy my faith as an Episcopalian. It might be a wonderful idea however, if Madeleine took classes. She has never been confirmed," said Punkin.

This compromise soothed Giselle for the moment, but then she was on to something bigger.

"*Je vous en prie*, Punkin, but what kind of name is Punkin? I have always thought it so odd," Giselle said as she buttered her cereal roll.

Punkin determined to stay calm.

"It was my mother's name and I am proud to claim it. She got the nickname when she was a child."

"Don't you have any other names?"

"My middle name is Elizabeth."

"*Eh bien* that is who you will be when you marry. Madame Elizabeth Aumont," Giselle said as if the decision had been made.

A lot of thoughts went through Punkin's mind at that moment. She had heard stories about French mothers-in-law and their control. Damn if she was going to cow-tow to this old bag. Diplomacy reigned, and Punkin replied in her most genteel Southern voice.

"Giselle, dear, that is a very pretty title, but it is not my name. I was even thinking about being Madame Punkin Lowery Aumont."

The waiter had just come to take their lunch order. It gave everyone time to gather their thoughts. Madeleine and Jean had remained quiet during the conversation. Neither of them wanted to get in the middle of it. Orders were taken, and Punkin and Giselle continued.

"The bride in France never keeps her own name. It is just not done in the better families," said Giselle.

Punkin turned her steely gaze on Jean and said,

"*Mon cher*, what do you think?"

Jean, ever the diplomat, said,

"*Mamie*, you know by now that American women are very independent, especially our Punkin."

"Giselle, do not take me wrong. I will be proud to be an Aumont, but I am also proud of my family name, too."

"I think Punkin should make her own decision, as I will when I marry. I may decide to keep the Aumont name, since I haven't had it very long."

The table finally heard from Madeleine.

"*Mon dieu*, are you all crazy? What is a heritage, if not to retain it?"

Giselle looked as if she was going to have palpitations.

"Let's all enjoy our lunch and not talk about the wedding. As Punkin said, I still have to find a suitable place for us to live in Paris," said Jean.

That did not calm Giselle down, and she got more agitated.

"I assumed you all would live with me in the family chateau. Jean is learning the business, and must be there on a regular basis. It has been our home for four generations."

Punkin was going to let Jean handle this one.

"*Chere maman*, Madeleine is young and her artistic career is just beginning. I would not expect my daughter to be buried in the provinces at her age."

"That's right Giselle. Madeleine's classes at the *Ecole des Beaux Arts* are going so well that her professor wants to put on an *exposition* of her work," said Punkin.

"*Grand-mere*, I love you, but Papa and Punkin are right. I have to stay in Paris, but of course will continue to visit you often," said Madeleine

Their lunch arrived. It gave them a good excuse to quit talking. No one seemed to have much of an appetite.

CHAPTER 4

Make-up Sex is the Best

The long anticipated family lunch ended as soon as the café had been finished. Nothing else was said about the wedding. Madeleine tried to entertain her family to break some of the tension. She told funny stories about her fellow art students at the *Ecole*. Those went over like a lead balloon.

Jean took his mother back to his apartment where she would spend the night before returning to home to the chateau the next morning. He settled her in, and then hurriedly drove to 9 *rue st. peres*. He knew his little *americaine* was not happy. Bless her heart, in the 18 months she had lived in Paris she had learned a lot. She loved France as much as Jean. However, this hierarchy system of the bourgeoise families, took much getting used to. She loved the "concept" of France but maybe not the reality. Nothing would be changed overnight, even by this dynamic Texan!

He arrived at 9 *rue st. peres*, punched in the door code, and then the code for the interphone, and took the elevator to the 4th floor. Rather than letting himself in, he gently knocked. He heard Madeleine, followed by Maurice and Babette, hurrying to the door. The dogs' little barks meant company was coming, and they were excited. Madeleine opened the door.

"*Salut* Papa," she said, as she gave him a hug.

They went into the living room. Jean could see Punkin standing in the kitchen at the sink washing dishes. Her back was to the door, and she did not acknowledge his arrival.

"*Ma fille*, would you take the dogs out for a little walk? I want to talk to Punkin", Jean said

Madeleine understood, quickly got their leashes, and they were out the door. Punkin had still not moved from the sink. He gently went up behind her, put his arms around her, turned her face to his and gave her a lingering kiss. At first, she resisted, but then returned it passionately.

"Well, that lunch was kind of a bust."

Punkin put down her dish towel and turned to face Jean.

"Sorry *cherie* but you know when Giselle gets something on her mind, she doesn't give up. Kind of reminds me of you. The two of you are exactly alike."

This was something Punkin did not want to hear. She was in a foul enough mood already.

They walked into the living room and sat down on the sofa. It had seen better days, and had a small spring sticking out of one corner.

"But, really, I am sorry. She is your mother, but who does she think she is to ask me to change my name? I thought the monarchy ended a long time ago."

Jean laughed. For some reason at this moment he was very aroused and getting a mighty erection. Without answering, he took Punkin's hand and put it on his crotch. A look of surprise and delight came over her face as she unzipped his pants to let the big boy out. She started to gently put his member in her mouth, but he stopped her.

"*Cherie*, I am about to burst. I need to be inside you now."

In seconds, he had her panties off and had entered her. He spread her wide and was thrusting so hard, they almost fell off the couch. They didn't even consider that Madeleine might walk in at any moment. In fact, that idea got them more excited.

Jean could always bring Punkin to a gigantic orgasm. Sebastian, the Count, although a good lover, did not have the know-how to get to the right spot to put Punkin into ecstasy.

They both came, and lay panting, their clothes all askew.

At that moment, they heard the key in the lock, and rapidly rearranged their clothes. Maurice, Babette and Madeleine came into the living room. The dogs and she could detect the smell of sex.

"What have you two been doing?"

Madeleine smiled. She certainly knew the answer to that question.

"Papa and Punkin were just having a discussion about your *grand-mere*."

"Oh, is that what you call it?"

Madeleine laughed and they did, too. In France, sex is just a natural part of life. Madeleine loved to see her "parents" happy after a stressful day.

Punkin got up from the couch rearranging her hair.

"Anybody hungry? I sure am, since I didn't eat much lunch."

Both Jean and Madeleine agreed they could eat something. Punkin first wanted to take a shower, and change into comfortable clothes.

"Why not let me cook, *mon amour?*"

Jean decided it was the least he could do after the disastrous lunch. He was a gourmet cook, in addition to his other capabilities.

"*Merveilleux*, I will be right back. I think there is a bottle of champagne in the frigo. Let's celebrate just the three of us being together," said Punkin.

Madeleine followed her father into the kitchen which was the biggest room in the apartment. It had a wonderful gas stove, a bar with stools for dining, a large cooking island for prep and serving, and a picture window, which looked out on the courtyard with its chestnut trees and flowers.

Madeleine got out the champagne and Jean started looking for something to prepare. Only things in the fridge were eggs, cheese, shallots, *crème fraiche* and some big strawberries. The girls had bought them at the *Marche Bio* on *boulevard Raspail*.

Jean decided on cheese omelettes with fresh shallots. They would have the strawberries for dessert. Jean would add a little *Grand Marnier* to the *crème*. It would be a simple meal, but a delicious one. In Paris, no one ever had to eat processed foods. There was such an abundance of fresh fruits, cheeses, vegetables, meats and poultry that came in from the countryside every morning. Paris was full of fabulous open markets, where something you bought would have just been off the vine for 24 hours.

Punkin joined them in the kitchen, glowing from good sex, a hot shower, and fresh clothes. She smelled the butter and shallots cooking in the pan.

"Oh I love omelettes. They are a perfect light dinner."

She and Madeleine settled on bar stools sipping their champagne while Jean cooked. Both Maurice and Babette hovered at Jean's feet, enticed by the great smell of eggs and onions cooking in good French butter.

"Since we have been talking about the wedding, maybe I should start calling you *maman*. Would that please you?"

Madeleine touched Punkin's arm and smiled.

Punkin felt a tear coming on. She was overflowing with emotion from the lunch, the sex, and now this heartfelt, surprise offer.

"Oh my dearest girl, did you think you had to ask? I am your mother," said Punkin as she hugged her girl.

The omelettes almost done, Jean turned off the stove, covering the pan.

"Can I join in this?"

He came over to give the two of them a group hug. The dogs, barking their approval, jumped into Madeleine's lap.

"Ok you two, *silence*, or you will not get any of our dinner."

Punkin petted them both on their heads.

Jean, Madeleine and Punkin sat at the bar drinking, eating their omelettes with crunchy French bread, and laughing about nothing. The discussion of Madame Elizabeth Aumont or Punkin Lowery Aumont was totally forgotten. It had turned out to be a great Sunday.

CHAPTER 5

Les Ecoles des Beaux Arts
Madeleine, the Art Student

Madeleine Junot Aumont was indeed the budding *artiste*. Damien Hunter's introduction to professional art at his studio in *Montmartre* was only the start. He knew she had enough talent to qualify for classes at the prestigious *Les Ecoles des Beaux Arts*. This renowned academy had been founded in 1682 and happily was right down the street from *rue st. peres* at 14 *rue Bonaparte*. Famous artists through the centuries had taken classes there like Edgar Degas, Constantin Brancusi, and Jean Charles Bonnard.

Madeleine was learning life drawing with live models, the use of oils, pastels and water colors, and how to give her work prospective. Her innate ability rapidly emerged with the right teachers. One in particular, *Monsieur Abadie*, the *chef d'Atelier* for first year students saw real promise in Madeleine. He wanted to display her work in the yearly exhibition of top students, which would be held in the fall.

The *Ecole* was expensive, and Jean was paying for her classes. Some of her fellow students were not as lucky. Art was as important as life to these students and they saved every dime, sometimes going without eating, to pay for their classes. Madeleine had befriended one of these students named Sophie.

She was a frail little thing, about Madeleine's age. The student gossip was that she lived in the most deplorable conditions in the 20th *arrondissement* of Paris. At their lunch breaks, the school provided café and *the*, but nothing else. Madeleine noticed that Sophie usually just brought an apple. She knew the girl was hungry, and started to bring extra food from home to share with Sophie. At first, she was too proud to accept it.

The sad thing was that her art was not that good. The art students in the beginner's class wondered how she had qualified in the first place. Sophie was determined to make it as an artist. A strong will could go a long way into making that a reality.

Another one of the students, Jacques, had a crush on Madeleine. He was 24, but seemed much younger. He was quite shy and not very good looking, with bad acne that covered most of his face, and hair that looked like it had been cut with a butcher knife. It stuck up all over his head in little clumps. He was a fairly promising student and *Monsieur Abadie's* encouragement was giving him confidence.

Antoine was the star of the class, and he knew it. He was also courting Madeleine's affections, but she thought him too arrogant. He was tall, patrician looking, with wavy blonde hair he was very proud of. He dressed in an odd style, emulating a fop of the 19th century. One of his heros had been the writer, Oscar Wilde. Wilde had coincidentally lived and died right down the street at l'Hotel. During Wilde's time, it had been mediocre and run-down, but now was a stylish boutique hotel for tourists. Antoine, of course, thought he knew more than *Monsieur Abadie*.

Madeleine and Punkin were still keeping in touch with Damien. Punkin had so loved the portrait he did of Madeleine, that she had commissioned him to do a portrait of herself. She would give it to Jean as a surprise wedding present.

CHAPTER 6

Paris is a Birthday

Spring was speeding along. Punkin's 52nd birthday was approaching in May. She wasn't happy about the numbers growing larger on the calendar, but living in Paris was joyous. Every day was a birthday.

In her almost 2 years in Paris, Punkin's circle of friends had grown. They were all interesting characters like Madeleine's art student *confreres* at the *Ecole des Beaux Arts*. Punkin's group, which varied from 5 to 20 on any given Sunday, gathered at the famed *Café de Flore* on the *Blvd St Germain* for a kind of *salon*, emulating those historic literary functions at an elegant home in the 17th and 18th centuries. We now call them a cocktail party.

You never knew who would show up. There would always be someone interesting like an author, an actor, or even a few reactionary Communists! They were a good mix of American and French. This merry band was led by a unique individual named Barney. Originally from Brooklyn, and still retaining a strong New Yorkese accent, he was loud, bombastic and just a whole lot of fun. One of the mainstays of the group was a mysterious French woman who never took off a large hat or dark sunglasses. They completely covered her face. Everyone chattered away in both English and French. Their *Flore* waiter, Chin, originally from Shanghai, kept the wine flowing.

Punkin was happy for this diversion on Sundays. Make-up sex with Jean or no, he was still being a pill. Men know no boundaries with women. They will take a mile if you let them. The right woman can make that distance an inch. Punkin was the right woman for

Jean. She just had to get past Giselle. Being more independent from Jean and making a good life for herself was the best way to proceed.

Besides growing a year older, Punkin's inheritance from her mother was gone. She had spent the last of it on 6 month's rent on the present apartment and to pay Damien for the portrait he was doing to give to Jean. That is, if the wedding ever happened.

Her lawyer, dear George Castellane, had gently suggested she find a job. He thought real estate might be a good *metier* for her. Punkin had made a successful living in the States in advertising and marketing. One had to be a good salesperson in that profession, and real estate was all about selling the right apartment to a willing buyer.

Through the American Club, she had met a *distinguee* Frenchman named Armand de Guissac.

He had an agency in the 7th *arrondissement* behind the *Assemble Nationale*, the French Congress. He only catered to the "carriage trade" of wealthy French and well- to- do international buyers. Punkin knew lots of rich Americans who loved Paris as she did. She was going to set up an interview with Armand and pitch like mad that he needed an American agent to find American clients.

CHAPTER 7

Agente Immobiliere

Punkin the Real Estate Agent

Punkin's interview was set right before the Easter holidays. Armand would have more time to visit with her, as most people were already leaving on vacation. She dressed in all her finery, and hoped her French was now good enough. The interview would only be conducted in the language of the country.

They met at his office on a warmish day. Punkin hoped she wouldn't sweat! Very few office buildings in Paris had *climatisation*, air conditioning. She began to talk, and it was beneficial that she knew Armand socially. She sensed he thought her pretty. After about 30 minutes of questions and answers, she was in.

Her position would be as a *travailleur independante* as the other agents were. This meant she was a consultant and would work under contract. She did not need to have a real estate license. In France, only the *gerant*, manager of the business, needed a license. Her job would be to bring in American clients and then participate in the commissions. On large sales of over 1 million euros she would make a good return, but would have to pay the tax on her commission to the French government. The French never missed an opportunity to collect taxes!

She would start the second week of April, after the holiday, and work with three other agents in the office on *rue de beaune*. They were all French, and men. Madeleine was excited for her, and Jean was impressed she would be working for a French agency- the snob! Work was always therapeutic for Punkin. It would take her mind off her troubles. Jean would have to take his rides in the *Bois de Boulogne* alone but *tant pis*, too bad.

She dressed in her best corporate American style for her first day. She wore a navy-blue linen suit from Brooks Brothers, a crisp white blouse, an *Hermes* scarf, and her *Roger Vivier* pumps with heels not too high. Showings of apartments were not done by car like in the U.S., but on foot. Wearing comfortable shoes was a must.

She arrived at the office promptly at 9am. Armand kissed her on both cheeks and showed her to her desk. She had a brand-new computer, but with a French keyboard. This *clavier* had the numbers and letters in a different configuration from the American *QUERTY* keyboard. Oh well, she was a fast learner. Armand introduced her to her fellow agents.

There was Alexander, a sharp young man of about 30. He was dressed in a double-breasted pin-stripe suit, with his short black hair slicked back with gel. He looked more Italian than French. The second agent, Patrick, was about 40 and a real *aristo*. He had that *bourgeoise* disdain for anyone who he thought not of his class. Punkin knew immediately that she would like him least. The third agent, Claude, the oldest of the three, was close to Punkin's age. He was the most experienced agent. She figured that she could learn a lot from him. Claude had a pleasing, friendly demeanor which might mean he would be willing to teach her.

There is no MLS, Multiple Listing Service, in France. Unlike the more efficient *etats-unis,* there is no master computerized list for apartments for sale in Paris in all locations and price ranges. Each agency had their own listings or *mandats* and guarded them like gold. Because there are so few listings per agency, agents in the same office are jealous of their fellow workers. They were determined to get a piece of any sale even if they had not done any work on a particular listing.

On this first day, to Punkin's consternation, everyone arrived on time, but then immediately decided to go out for *café*. This left the office unattended. Punkin had eaten her breakfast, and drunk her coffee, and was ready to work. She quickly learned in the weeks that followed, this was the routine. The office would open, then they would go for coffee, come back to the office for an hour or two and work on their computers or answer the phones. Then at 1pm they would go to lunch. Lunch in France always lasted at least 2 hours, so ½ of the day was gone without anything concrete being accomplished.

Once a week, one of the agents stayed at the office over lunch to answer calls and record prospects in a big red, leather-bound book. Punkin diligently recorded every call, what the prospective client wanted, and their phone number. She reported these prospects at their annual weekly meeting, but she was the only agent who ever called anyone back. How, she wondered did any agents ever make a sales commission?

She had been on the job about one month, when a great opportunity dropped in her lap. She had met a couple from New York at an American Club cocktail and came to find out they were renting a large apartment right down the street from her office. They expressed an interest in buying, and their budget of 1.5 million euros was legitimate. This might mean a good commission for Punkin even if she had to share it with the *gerent*, and also pay the tax.

Our little Texan got to work in researching all that was available at the office and also contacting other agencies to see what was in their portfolios.

It was real luck, but she found the perfect apartment in the 8th *arrondissement*. She took the couple to see it and they loved it. They were ready to make an offer for almost full price and wanted a quick closing so they could move out of their rental. Punkin, all excited, presented their offer to Armand. She had done all the paperwork correctly and mentioned to Armand that they wanted a quick closing.

Another holiday was coming up in early May, which meant most French would be away for two weeks.

In Punkin's opinion, the French took more holidays-religious or school related- than any country she knew of. She calculated, amusingly, that with all these holidays, the French actually only worked about 5 months per year. You could also forget about July and August when everyone took a 6-week vacation.

When the other agents got wind of this potential sale, they hovered around Punkin like sharks in a feeding frenzy, all trying to justify how they each helped her with her clients. The truth was that they had done *rien*, nothing, to make this sale happen.

Armand looked at the proposed date of the closing and with a straight, serious face told Punkin that it was out of the question because he was going on vacation. Punkin in her shock and dismay, tried to explain that in America, for a big commission/sale in hand, a vacation would certainly be postponed. Armand wouldn't budge.

Punkin knew it was no use to argue with a Frenchman. Any confrontation and they became like a trapped animal. Kind of like the "deer in the headlights" syndrome. She tried to cajole him, and said she would be happy to keep the office open for this transaction. He was having none of it, and casually added that maybe their association was not working out

It was the end of Punkin's career as an *agente immobiliere* in Paris.

CHAPTER 8

Co-Habitation

Making money in real estate was out. Punkin was beginning to stress badly about money. It was making her physically sick, and she couldn't sleep at night. Jean had been promising for months to find an apartment for the three of them and the time needed to be now. Right after Punkin's birthday, the lease on *st. peres* would be up. She would either have to ask Jean for money or they all would need to be in an apartment that Jean would pay for. He was already supporting Madeleine, but she didn't want to beg him for her support, too. Punkin was proud. That pride might be getting in her way.

Since she was now un-employed, she was free once again to ride in the *Bois* with Jean. Her horse, Chiquita Banana, the beautiful Palomino mare Jean had given her at Christmas, was stabled at his club, *Polo de Paris*. He rode her from time to time, but preferred to ride his own horse, a black stallion named Stormy. Chiquita needed a good work out and so did Punkin.

A brisk ride in the *Bois* would be the perfect time to talk. The weather would be getting too warm in June and July to keep riding on a regular basis.

Jean came over for dinner every night, but with Madeleine around, there was no time for the adults to talk. Punkin never wanted to disturb the father/daughter time. It was so pleasant for her to see the two of them together. Their facial expressions, movements and sense of humor were so the same. The three of them had been discussing what to do for Punkin's birthday in a couple of weeks, but our Texas/Paris girl was not in a celebratory mood.

To take her mind off her troubles, she decided to cook a grand meal for the three of them. She loved to cook and found it so relaxing. She made a pretty good *cassoulet*, the white bean, duck, sausage and chicken casserole famous in southwestern France. This recipe was said to have originated in the town of *Toulouse*. She shopped all day for the ingredients going to the *boucherie* for the meats and the market on *Raspail* for the beans and seasonings. It would be an all-day cooking process.

The weather was again a little warm for the end of April. There was no air-conditioning in the apartment. The stove and oven overheated her making Punkin a little irritable. Plus, the *cassoulet* was turning out a bit dry. She had been drinking white wine all afternoon and was almost drunk when Madeleine returned from art school.

"Oh, something smells good!" Madeleine hugged her soon- to-be her official mother.

Punkin returned the hug, but Madeleine could tell she was a little "frazzled".

"I hope your papa likes the *cassoulet*. He is so particular about everything being just perfect," said Punkin.

Madeleine looked at her with the wise eyes of a 21-year old. "*Maman, n'inquietez pas*, Papa loves anything you do."

"At least our first course will be OK. I found the most wonderful smoked salmon and we will have it with capers, lemon and *crème fraiche*."

Punkin hurried off to shower and change.

Jean arrived at 7pm. Her shower had sobered Punkin up a bit, and she felt more calm. She had dressed in flowing palazzo pants, flats, and a Pucci print blouse. Because it was so hot, she put her hair up in a *chignon*. She completed her outfit with long dangling earrings from India in silver and turquoise.

"*Bonsoir* my girls," Jean said as he kissed them both.

"My, you look nice," he said admiring his love.

Punkin poured him a glass of Aumont *grand cru* red, and put out some olives and nuts. She poured Madeleine and herself glasses of their favorite white.

"What a marvellous smell. It that *cassoulet*? Toulouse where it is famous, is so close to Bordeaux, I love that dish. *Maman* fixed it often," he said.

Here we go, thought Punkin. She would even have to compete with Giselle in the kitchen.

"*Cheri*, it might not be as good as your mother's. I think it got a little too dry, but we have some succulent smoked salmon to start."

"I want to hear all about your day at the real estate office," said Jean.

"Been meaning to tell you, I quit. It is too long a story to tell over dinner. I thought we might take a ride this week in the *Bois* and I could tell you all about it. I want to talk to you about some other things, too," Punkin said as she led them to the dining table.

"I do not know why you quit your job. However, I am happy to have you around during the day so we can ride again. Chiquita has really missed you," Jean said as he seated himself at the head of the table.

Punkin should have left it alone, but she didn't.

"Let's just say quitting my job was necessary. No offence to your countrymen, but they do not do business as we Americans do."

Punkin's agitation was coming back.

"What do you mean?"

Jean had a defensive look on his face that Punkin had not seen often.

Madeleine could sense the tension between her parents.

"This salmon is *merveilleux*. I can not wait to taste the *cassoulet*," Madeleine said

Punkin was fed up, stressed and drunk.

"I might as well tell you, Jean Aumont, that I think French business people are idiots. I brought the agency some wonderful clients who were ready to buy. I had them eating out of my hand until my boss said he couldn't be bothered to finish the deal because he was going on vacation. I lost a big commission, my job, and am totally broke."

All this spilled out in one long sentence. Madeleine and Jean stopped eating and just looked at her.

"What does that mean exactly? Will we have to move from here?"

Madeleine had that same sad agitated look on her face that Punkin had first noticed when they met. That was a time when no one wanted Madeleine.

"No, not if your father will finally make the arrangements for us to live together and pay for it."

As soon as Punkin said this she was sorry. She had not meant to get into any of this tonight.

"Sweetness, I had no idea things had gotten so bad for you financially. I will start looking for an apartment for us tomorrow."

"Tomorrow? You have had more than 3 months to find us a place. Since you are retired, I assume you have nothing else to do," Punkin said with a sneer.

Jean looked hurt and surprised. Punkin recanted.

"I am sorry, precious. I have had a long hot day cooking this meal for the two people I love most in the world. I know you will do your best and not let us down. This lease ends in one month."

Jean, only slightly appeased said, "One month, *trente jours*, that doesn't give me much time."

"Well, I guess then we will have to move into your tiny place. I am really up against it, and need your help!"

"Or do you have to ask your mother's permission first?"

Punkin was not doing herself any favors.

Jean looked at them both, quietly got up from the table, and left. Paris Perfect, my ass!

CHAPTER 9

Down to the Tabourette

As the old Southern expression goes, Punkin was "fit to be tied". After Jean walked out, there was nothing Madeleine could do to calm her down. All the frustration, anger, and uncertainty about her future exploded. This nice Texas girl had to do something bad.

It was now around 10pm. Punkin had another drink, this time a big tumbler of scotch. Madeleine had never seen her sweet friend behave this way, and it frightened her. The daughter was now becoming the mother. She must figure a way to diffuse this situation and protect Punkin from herself.

"*Maman, calme-toi*. Papa will certainly be back. He loves us so. Why don't you have a little more to eat? You are going to feel terrible in the morning."

"*Non*, I tell you what I want to do. I am going to the Tabourette."

Madeleine knew the Tabourette well. She and Marcel had been there often late at night. It was an all-night *tabac/café* that somehow got permission from the City of Paris to serve drinks all night. She and Marcel had often stayed until daylight, picking up tricks for Madeleine. She remembered grimly those times, and seeing the Tabourette staff hose down the bar between 6 and 7am for the new arrivals. It was a place that anything could happen, and often did.

"*Maman*, surely you do not want to go to the Tabourette. There are criminals there!"

Madeleine never wanted Punkin to experience that seamy side of life that Madeleine had finally escaped, thanks to Punkin.

"Why not? My life at the moment is shit. I need to cut loose."
Punkin added,

"Of course, *cherie*, you can go with me, but I do not want to remind you of old memories."

"You will not leave this apartment without me!"

Madeleine stomped her foot. Babette and Maurice, who had been sleeping in the bedroom, scurried out hearing the loud voices and Madeleine's heavy foot on the wood floor.

"Put the dogs back in the bedroom and close the door. I am calling G7 taxi to pick us up."

Punkin would not be swayed.

Madeleine was filled with fear. The Tabourette was a hang-out of Marcel's and she had heard he was out of prison. She trembled at the thought of what she might do to him if he crossed their paths again. What he had done to her was horrific. He had stolen her youth, and she did not know how she would ever have sex with a man she loved. He had ruined that for her.

The taxi arrived quickly, and Madeleine steadied Punkin into the cab.

"Tabourette, *s'il vous plait. Est ce que vous le connaissez* –do you know it ? "

The driver, a young man of about Madeleine's age, looked at the two of them in a queer way, shrugged his shoulders and said *oui*. Off they went for the 15-minute ride into the *centre ville*. The Tabourette was located behind the *gare st lazare*, not a particularly good part of town.

When they arrived, crowds were spilling out of the Tabourette onto the sidewalk in all forms of intoxication. Most of them were idling, smoking cigarettes. It was an odd mix of North Africans, models, actors and a few couples from the better parts of town, "slumming". Then Madeleine saw Marcel.

Thankfully, the crowd outside was so large, he did not see them. Madeleine grabbed Punkin, kept her head down and guided Punkin into the bar. Inside was worse than outside. The place smelled of stale beer and sweat. Madeleine cleared the way to the two remaining stools at the bar.

"Whiskey," Punkin said slapping down a 20 euro note on the bar.

"*Un coca lite pour moi, merci,*" said Madeleine

Madeleine ordered a coke. She had to stay very sober this night. There was a jukebox in the corner playing Piaf.

"*Ma chere*, take this change and find some Sinatra. I am tired of this French crap," slurred Punkin.

The next tune up was the Stones, *You Can't Always Get What You Want*. How appropriate, Punkin mused. The shot of whiskey arrived, she gulped it down and and veered onto the dance floor. Punkin was a good dancer, and dancing by herself was not a problem. All the booze had lowered her inhabitations to zero. Several couples joined her on the dance floor. She was making such a spectacle of herself, they stopped to watch her, clapping to the beat.

The noise brought some of the outdoor crowd back into the bar. One of them was Marcel.

He still had not seen Madeleine, but recognized Punkin. He would never forget the bitch who had put him away after that Thanksgiving confrontation at the apartment on *Avenue President Wilson*. He had a score to settle. Marcel approached Punkin.

"*Dancez, Madamemoiselle?*"

Punkin froze. She was instantly sober. She could never forget those black, piercing eyes, spiked hair and the palpable feeling of pure evil that surrounded him. She turned to walk off the dance floor, looking with plaintive eyes in Madeleine's direction. Marcel followed her gaze and finally saw Madeleine. He grabbed Punkin's arm dragging her back to the bar.

"*Eh bien, mes putaines*, what luck. I have been looking for you, but never thought I would find you here," hissed Marcel.

Madeleine stood up and slapped him across the face.

"Leave my mother alone!"

The slap exacerbated Marcel's anger, and he pulled out his knife lunging at Madeleine. With a mother's instinct, Punkin blocked the blow and the knife slashed through her hand. Blood was everywhere, and someone in the crowd screamed. The bartender quickly jumped over the bar and restrained Marcel, helped by two other men.

Punkin was in shock. The *SAMU*, paramedics were called and arrived quickly. Punkin needed 12 stitches to close the wound. She and Madeleine were put in the van to go to the nearest hospital emergency room. Punkin was patched up with great care at a very small cost, even for an emergency room.

Punkin was heavily sedated, and she and Madeleine got into another cab to go back to the safety of *rue st. peres*. This was a wake-up call for Punkin. She realized how lucky she was. Madeleine put her to bed, and returned to the living room to have a strong drink of her own.

The *gendarmes* had taken Marcel to jail, but he would only be held overnight since they had not pressed charges. The most important thing had been to get Punkin to the hospital.

Madeleine thought for a long time sitting and drinking until dawn. She was determined to make sure Marcel would pay for all he had done. She just wasn't sure how to do it. She would figure out a plan, so he would never bother them or anyone else ever again.

CHAPTER 10

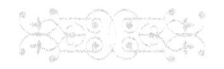

Trauma

Punkin woke at 6am with the sound of her cell phone ringing. Coming out of her sleep fog, she assumed it must be Jean calling. She realized her head was aching and her hand was throbbing. She looked at her bandaged hand, and it all came back to her. Geez Punkin, she said softly to herself. You have fucked up big time.

She had no desire to talk to Jean this morning, until her head cleared a bit. She looked across at Madeleine's bed and no Madeleine. Punkin kind of remembered coming home with her, but where was she? Getting slowly out of bed she tip-toed into the living room. There on the lumpy couch was that angelic child sound asleep, the dogs surrounding her, sleeping peacefully, too.

Punkin needed a big cup of strong French café. She hoped the sound of the espresso machine would not wake her little family up. The dawn was breaking. Outside her kitchen window she saw the Paris sky, all pink and blue. God, she loved this country!

She had a real problem. With Marcel back in Paris and on the loose, they would never be safe here. She knew Jean and Madeleine would never let the incident pass without dire consequences. She didn't know what she would say to Jean. First and foremost, she was going to apologize for her rotten behaviour. She was lucky to have him, and glad to be alive.

Maybe Giselle was right. Should they move to Bordeaux? Moving to the chateau would not be best for Madeleine's art career, but it was Jean's home, and Madeleine did love her grand mother.

Living in the quiet of Bordeaux would give Madeleine a little of her childhood back. It would, in addition, solve the problem of where they were going to live, and Marcel could never get to them there.

Punkin had exactly 500 euros left in her bank account. Her rent was 1500 euros per month. There was no way to make money to keep them there. The more she thought about it, she cheered up. Jean would be happy because his mother would be happy, and Punkin would just have to deal with being Madame Aumont *dans les provinces*, in the small town, that was Bordeaux.

The sound of the coffee machine jarred her out of her reverie. It also roused the dogs and dear Madeleine.

"*Maman*, you are up."

Madeleine and the dogs untangled from the sofa and the duvet to come into the kitchen. Punkin noticed Madeleine's puffy eyes. She had either been crying or not gotten much sleep. Punkin hugged her and could feel her body still warm from the duvet.

"*Cherie*, I was concerned when I didn't see you in your bed this morning."

"After I put you to bed, I decided to have my own drink. I guess I fell asleep on the couch."

Punkin knew Madeleine wanted to talk about last evening. She took control and steered the conversation.

"Last night was a nightmare, and I apologize. I can not remember ever having that much to drink."

"You scared me. And then, what were the chances of running into Marcel? I want to kill him, and Papa will, too, when he hears about it."

"*Ca suffit*, enough about that. I do not want you saying anything to your father. I will do the talking, and will mention nothing about Marcel."

"Say nothing about Marcel? He is the reason you have 12 stitches in you hand!"

"We will say that I had too much to drink, and I had convinced you to take me to the Tabourette. He knows how bad that place is. This could have easily happened with someone breaking a bottle or a glass and my being caught in the middle of it."

Madeleine looked confused but would defer to her mother and elder. Punkin decided to broach the subject of Bordeaux.

"How would you feel about living in Bordeaux with *mamie*?"

"You mean all three of us, right? I don't know. I was born in Paris and have made some good friends at the *Ecole*. What about my exhibition? I have worked so hard, and Professor Abadie is so proud of me."

"I know *mon ange*. You have been so diligent in your art studies. When is the exhibition?"

"Not until September."

Madeleine looked very small and vulnerable. She was looking into her mother's eyes for some answer.

"Let me talk to your father, and see what we can work out. The first thing is, he and I have to get married. Your *grand-mere* will be happy to make all the arrangements. It will be fun."

Punkin said this with the realization that life demands compromises. Living in Bordeaux with a mother-in-law she detested, would be hers to protect her child and her husband.

"And don't forget, we have to celebrate your birthday first," Madeleine said, cheering up a bit herself.

Punkin knew she and Jean were planning something special for her birthday. That would take their minds off Marcel. They drank their strong cups of coffee, dunking their *croissants* in the big coffee bowls.

"Will you take the dogs out for their walk? I need to return your father's calls."

CHAPTER 11

Apologies

It was now 8:30am and Jean had been calling for hours. Punkin had purposely left her cell phone in the bedroom. She was now ready to deal with Jean. She tapped his number into the phone with her left hand. Marcel had damaged her writing hand, and it would be difficult for a while to do daily tasks. She would talk to Jean, apologize, say all was well. After that, she would take a big dose of Advil and go back to bed.

Jean picked up immediately. He sounded anxious.

"My love, are you OK? I called several times last night after I left and no answer. Sorry about walking out like that."

"Yes, my love, Madeleine and I are fine. The person who needs to apologize is me."

There was a momentary silence on the phone. Both of them were quietly gathering their thoughts. They began to speak at the same time.

"I love you."

They said it in unison, and then both laughed.

"You first," said Jean

"After you left, I unfortunately got real drunk, and dragged Madeleine to the Tabourette with me."

"Not the Tabourette. I don't believe it. That is a horrible place!"

"I have no idea why I wanted to go there. It seemed like a good idea at the time. I am sure it was the booze talking."

Punkin was trying to keep the conversation light. She was leading into her lie about her damaged hand. She continued.

"And unfortunately, I cut my hand rather badly there."

"What?"

"You know the Tabourette, always lots of crazies late at night. A bottle flew across the room, landed on the bar where we were sitting. It exploded into a million pieces right into my hand."

There, the lie was told.

"*Ma pauvre*, is your hand pretty bad?"

"I needed several stitches, but the SAMU fixed me right up. We went to the emergency room at a nearby hospital, don't ask me which. Then Madeleine and I took a taxi home."

"Thank God you all are all right. Please tell me you will never do that again."

"Believe me, I won't. Since it is my right hand, I will not be able to do much for a couple of weeks."

"*Cherie*, don't worry about that. Madeleine and I will help you. I will start looking for apartments immediately. Sorry I have been so slow."

Here was the next difficult subject to address.

"I have been thinking about our living quarters. Maybe your mother is right. Bordeaux might be a perfect place to live."

"I thought you hated Bordeaux."

Jean sounded a little confused.

"I know I said that, but it might be grand for the three of us to get a fresh start in your hometown."

"Why do you have this sudden change of heart?"

Jean was a little suspicious and Punkin lied harder.

"You are so involved now in the wine business, and I know it is hard to commute back and forth. Plus, wine making is an interesting profession. Maybe I could learn it, too."

"Do you really mean it?"

"Yes, I would feel like a princess living in 600 square meters of a grand chateau instead of 100 square meters in a Paris apartment. But, Giselle must let me be Punkin Aumont, not Elizabeth."

Punkin could sense Jean smiling in the phone.

"This is wonderful news. I never thought you would agree. I was willing to keep us here to make you and Madeleine happy. Living in Bordeaux makes much more sense. Have you discussed this with Madeleine?"

"Already done and she is OK about it. She loves her grandmother. We just need to figure a way for her to continue her art. We also need to be in Paris in September for her exhibition."

"*D'accord*, there is just one more question," Jean said.

"When will you marry me?"

Now Punkin was smiling into the phone.

"*Monsieur*, I thought you would never ask. I think as soon as possible. I am sure Giselle is ready and willing to start the plans *tout de suite*.

"I am so happy, my dearest love. I will call *maman* right now. Will I see you all tonight?"

"*Bien sur*, come over around 6. Let's go out to someplace festive. We have a lot to be thankful for."

Punkin blew Jean a kiss into the phone, hung up, and immediately got back in bed.

CHAPTER 12

A Croisere and Wedding Plans

Being 52 was not turning out too bad. Punkin and Jean were back on track, and there was her birthday and a wedding to plan. Life was again moving at a fast, happy pace. Jean and Madeleine surprised Punkin with a private cruise on the *Seine* for her birthday and invited her best friends in Paris. George Castellane, her lawyer and the *grandes dames* of *Avenue President Wilson* were there as well as Tom and Eleanor Charleson (who had finally mended fences with her after the Thanksgiving debacle), plus Damian Hunter, her college friend and Madeleine's first art teacher, plus a nutty bunch of Madeleine's art student friends.

The *Croisiere* was a cocktail at sunset. It was a lovely May evening with a light breeze, blue skies and a big yellow sun sinking into the waters of the *Seine*. Jean hired a small band for dancing. Everybody got into the spirit of the old *guingettes*, dances on the river banks, which were popular in the 40's and 50's. The colored lights on the boat gave everyone a golden glow. Even Giselle had a good time. She held court telling the younger ones fascinating stories of the war years. She had a dance or two and was nimble on her feet. No one wanted the party to end.

Punkin's hand was much improved, but it was still a reminder of Marcel. She could not get him out of her mind, no matter how hard she tried. The wedding date had been set for the first weekend in June. She would be the proverbial June bride. Since this was her first (and hopefully) only marriage, she was pulling out all the stops. She would wear a white wedding dress, long veil and have bridesmaids. Madeleine would be maid of honor and Suzie Gilmore, matron of honor.

Giselle was in her element planning the wedding. She was thrilled to be part of the attention for the big day. The dean of the American Cathedral in Paris had agreed to do the ceremony in the Aumont family church is *St. Emilion*, and many of Jean and Punkin's friends were training down from Paris for the weekend. The civil ceremony, more legal in France than a religious one, would be in the town hall in Bordeaux on Friday.

The wedding and reception would be Saturday. The chateau would be the venue for the reception, a seated dinner amidst the vineyards.

Punkin had picked out the perfect dress. A slim sheath of *Alencon* lace and *duchesse* satin with an off the shoulder neckline that would show off her creamy shoulders and long blonde hair. At her slim waist, would be a band of dark green satin ribbon to accentuate her eyes.

Her bridesmaids would be dressed in deep red silk with white satin sashes. They would carry nosegays of pink and white roses.

Giselle surprised Punkin with the gift of her own wedding veil, exquisite lace from Bruges, Belgium. It was more than a meter long, and intricately beaded with seed pearls. It had been passed down to Giselle from her mother and her grandmother before that. Madeleine would wear it, too, on her wedding day.

The *vignerons*, winemakers, of the neighboring estates were invited. Renowned families from estates like Pichon- Longeville, Margaux and Lafitte would be there. These illustrious families had been in the wine business for centuries like the Aumonts. Punkin was hoping she would like the wives. This wine community was a tight one. She was nervous about fitting in and joining this incestuous group.

There was much to be done to leave *st. peres*, and Punkin was ready to get out of Paris. She was going into unfamiliar territory being an *haute bourgeoise* wife. She was dreading what she imagined as a more regimented life than the free-wheeling style of Paris.

Madeleine was being a real trooper. Punkin knew her little girl really didn't want to leave the *Ecole des Beaux Arts*, and all the progress she had made there. Professor Abadie used his connections to get her a private teacher in Bordeaux. She would continue working on her art for the exhibition in September. Jean and Punkin would have to squeeze this Paris visit in, as September was the *vendage*, grape harvest. It was important to get the grapes off the vines at just the right moment to create the best new *cru*. Worst case scenario was that Punkin would go with Madeleine to set up the show, and then Jean would follow for the actual event.

They had decided to keep Jean's *pied a terre*. They would use it for their frequent trips to Paris. Punkin hoped to occasionally escape Bordeaux for a day or two. Her light would be that she would still have Paris in case things got a little frantic in Bordeaux.

Besides planning the wedding, Giselle was remodelling the first floor of the chateau for improved living quarters for the three of them. Jean and Punkin would have a grand master suite with adjoining office for Jean. Giselle would still occupy her massive bedroom down the hall. Not much of a honeymoon with your mother-in-law within ear-shot.

Madeleine's rooms would be on the second floor. She would have an adjoining studio with large windows looking out on the vineyards, giving her lots of light for her painting and drawing.

CHAPTER 13

Leaving Paris and a Letter

The day finally arrived at the end of May to pack up and leave a life in Paris Punkin had started nearly two years before. She thought about her lost love in Houston. Alex's suicide and the death of her beloved mother only a few months later were the impetus for her to change her life and move to Paris. So much had happened in the last two years. She had her affair with the married count, Sebastian, had met Jean at the American Club along with her best friend, Suzie, and through her desire to do something good for someone else, had met her darling Madeleine.

Moving from *st. peres* was not at heart-wrenching as leaving *President Wilson*. She and Madeline had not had time to make the lasting friendships they had developed with their neighbors in the 16th. It wasn't a big move, since *st. peres* had come furnished. Jean rented a mini-van to take the family and the dogs to Bordeaux.

Right before they were getting ready to leave, a letter arrived. There was no return address but Madeleine instantly recognized Marcel's scrawl. She and Punkin opened the letter together. It was obscene and violent. Marcel wrote in excruciating detail what he was going to do sexually to both Madeleine and Punkin if he ever caught up with them. Neither of them could figure out how he had gotten their address.

They decided they would not tell Jean. It was better, since they were leaving Paris for good. Marcel could not possibly find them. They did think it wise, however, to file a report with the *Prefecture de Police*, and gave their new address in Bordeaux in case they had any additional news about Marcel. Punkin also called George and sent him a copy of the letter.

George had turned into a very good criminal lawyer and they might need him at some point. They both felt bad about lying to Jean. It was really eating on Punkin, but in the last two years in Paris she had learned it was best just to live day to day.

On a happier note, Punkin couldn't believe she was actually getting married, finally! Good things come to those who wait, as the old adage goes. They loaded up and left on a holiday, Pentecost, the last Monday in May, and also the celebration of Memorial Day in the U.S. The traffic was fairly heavy on the *auto route* with families heading out for *le pont*, a three-day weekend.

The weather was good, and both Madeleine and Punkin enjoyed seeing the countryside. France is such an agricultural country with miles of green fields and vegetation. There are also lots of cattle, which reminded Punkin of Texas. Babette and Maurice stretched their heads out the windows, feeling the breeze, on the three- hour trip to their new home.

CHAPTER 14

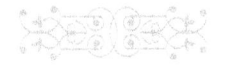

Chateau Aumont

The arrival in Bordeaux was liberating. They were 500 kilometres away from Marcel. As they drove up to the chateau, they were amazed by the sight. Lush green vines about to burst with plump red grapes. At the end of each row were blooming rose bushes. This was an old wine grower's trick, practiced for centuries. *Les vignerons* planted these beautiful bushes for the bugs to eat instead of the precious *raisins*.

Construction for the new addition was still going on, and Punkin was a bit concerned they would not be finished before the wedding in one week's time. Workmen were everywhere and the dust was terrible. However, Giselle seemed calm. She was freshly coiffed and perfumed and ready to greet her family. She had won, she thought. The family would all be together in this grand pile of a chateau, and she was determined to rule the roost.

Jean and Punkin would stay in separate rooms before the wedding. God bless Giselle, she was traditional to the last! He would be in his old room at the top of the house, and Madeleine and Punkin would share a small room down the hall from Giselle. Since the rest of the first floor and Madeleine's new rooms on the second floor were under renovation, they had no choice.

Giselle got them settled and then Jean and Punkin took a long walk into the vineyards. The sun was just setting and there was a wonderful smell of *terroir*, the earth, and things growing.

When they were far enough away from the house with no one to hear them, Jean said to Punkin.

"Ok, *ma chere*, I know something is wrong, and is troubling both my girls."

Punkin wasn't expecting this and had to think hard.

"Oh, I guess just the excitement of the trip, the wedding, and our new life here. It is such big change for both of us."

"I don't buy it. We are going to be man and wife in a week. That means your joy and sorrows are mine, too."

Jean kissed her gently, putting his arms around her, touching her face.

That was all it took. Punkin, so filled with emotion, had to tell Jean about the letter.

She told him all the gory details.

"My God, Punkin. You should have told me before we left Paris. I have some very influential friends that could make sure this pervert is put away for more than just a few months."

"Madeleine and I just didn't want to involve you. We thought you might do something violent. Even our sweet Madeleine says if she ever sees him again she will kill him. Let's concentrate on our happy future together and just forget it."

Punkin knew she could not forget it, and neither could Madeleine. For the time being they were safe. She wanted to change the subject.

"Tell me, almost husband of mine. What do you expect of this Texas girl as the wife of a grand wine grower? I don't have to dress like Giselle, do I?"

Jean was not in a joking mood.

"Punkin, I can not let this go. How could you be so irresponsible and just let this pass? Our honeymoon will have to wait. After we are married, I am going back to Paris and get a lawyer."

Jean said this with great agitation. Then Punkin let him have it.

"*D'accord*, I might as well tell you I am even more irresponsible. My cut hand did not come from a broken bottle at the Tabourette. Marcel was there, and lunged at me and Madeleine with a knife. To protect our little girl, I took the blow".

Now, the gloves were off.

"WHO am I marrying? I don't know you anymore. You seem to have gone from a nice girl from Texas to some kind of liar."

"What do you mean, some kind of liar? You are not a liar, but you are so weak! You can not even wipe your ASS without your mother's permission. If you think I am going to turn into her, and be a little dutiful winemaker's wife you are sadly mistaken."

When Punkin was rolling, her big mouth just kept going.

"And I do hate Bordeaux and all these in-bred families. The only reason I agreed to live here is to get away from Paris and the threat of Marcel. You have *aucune idée*, no idea, what he did to your little girl. I am surprised she is so normal under the circumstances."

"What do you mean?"

"He raped her, made her have sex with numerous men, and it took all the courage she could muster to get away from him. No surprise she wants to kill him. I do, too"

Punkin's green eyes were blazing, and she continued.

"Maybe we shouldn't get married. You are so fucking naïve. Who wants to be married to a mama's boy?"

Jean looked like he was going to hit her, and she was ready for a fight. He tried to grab her by her hurt hand and she pulled back, feeling the pain.

"Do not touch me! I am going back to the house, and you had better leave me alone for a while. This dream is turning into a nightmare."

With that, Punkin turned and stalked off through the wine fields back towards the house.

Jean watched her go with a tear in his eye. He could not move from the spot where he was standing.

CHAPTER 15

Down to the Stables

Punkin was stuck. She had no place to run, except maybe back to the U.S. That prospect was not appealing. It was either stay with Jean, Giselle, and Madeleine here in Bordeaux or nothing. When she got back to the house, thankfully, both Giselle and Madeleine were in their rooms dressing for dinner. She was so restless and disturbed she couldn't stay in the chateau. She decided to walk down to the stables to see Chiquita. She loved her little Palomino even more than she did Maurice. Petting and coddling her might calm her down.

Loic, the wine master, was in the stables when she arrived. Besides teaching Jean the art of wine making, he was also the major domo of the estate.

"Madame Punkin, it's late for you to be here, and too dark to take a ride," he said

"*Bonsoir* Loic. I just wanted to see how my little Chiquita made the trip down from Paris. Those trailers can be a bit confining for the horses."

"Oh, she is fine and so is Monsieur's horse, Stormy. Horses love to be in the fresh air and have lots of countryside to explore. She may be a little frisky the next time you ride her."

Punkin was happy to talk to Loic to take her mind off her argument with Jean. She loved the smell of fresh hay in the stables, mixed with the heady aroma of horse manure. Besides Chiquita and Stormy, there were several other riding horses, available to guests who frequently visited. The horses all "nayed" hello as she entered.

"I have never seen Monsieur Jean so happy. I have known him since he was a little boy. When his father died, he was so young, just 10 years old. It was so hard on him."

Punkin tried to imagine Jean as a small boy. Since he was such a tall, lanky adult, he must have been a little gangly as a child. She suspected he had always been taller than his schoolmates which might have made it difficult to make friends. Punkin knew that feeling. By the time she was 12, she had already reached her full height of 6 feet, and always felt self-conscious about it.

"Tell me more about his early life," she said

Loic continued.

"His grandfather, Etienne, as I am sure you know, was a grand military man. That is why Jean pursued the military as his career. Etienne was very strict and hard on Jean, especially after Jean's father died. *En plus*, Monsieur Etienne was always criticizing Madame Giselle for spoiling the boy and being too soft on him."

"Poor Jean," said Punkin

She was realizing for the first time that her love had not had an easy life either.

"Giselle did not want Jean to go into the military. She wanted him to be safe and sequestered at the chateau, and become a great vintner like his father."

"So I guess the grandfather won out," said Punkin

She was beginning to see Giselle's side of the story, too.

"*Oui*, Monsieur Etienne was very adamant and shipped Jean off to the *Ecole Militaire* in Paris as soon as they would take him. He was only 17 when he left the chateau."

"Didn't he at least get to come visit his mother from time to time?"

"*Non*, that is the sad part of it. His military training took four years, and then he was sent off to Algeria."

Sensing Loic knew more, Punkin decided to ask him about Rose, Madeleine's mother.

"Did you know anything about Jean's lost love, Rose?"

"Yes, we did indeed talk about her often, mostly in the letters he sent to me from Paris and Algeria."

"Then you know he never knew Rose was pregnant, or that he had a daughter?"

"Yes, that was quite sad. When he met you and then Madeleine, and discovered the truth, he was over the moon about it", Loic said with a big smile.

"You can not imagine, Madame Punkin, how the two of you have changed Jean's life for the better."

Punkin was getting the big picture. All of life's events are inter-connected, creating cause and effect, with either good or bad consequences. She saw clearly now for the first time that her chance encounter with Madeleine, her meeting Jean, and the grand surprise of Madeleine being his daughter all started with Punkin moving to Paris. She was the catalyst in this little family.

"*Merci bien Loic.* You were so kind to speak to me about all this tonight."

She embraced him, and he shyly smiled, looking embarrassed at this intimacy. He wasn't used to the *patrons* of the chateau being so familiar with the hired help.

"I must go back up to the chateau. My family may be worried about me, and I am so late for dinner!"

She said the word family as if she really meant it. These people of Chateau Aumont were her family. Punkin didn't need to go anyplace else. She was home.

CHAPTER 16

The Wedding Weekend

After Punkin returned to the house from the stables, dinner with Jean was extremely difficult. She felt awkward being around Giselle and Madeleine who had no idea what had transpired between the couple. Punkin had learned a lot about Jean from Loic, and after a good meal and lots of wine, the two decided to make up. After dinner, they snuck away to the fields to make love under the stars. They talked quietly a long time after and each agreed Marcel was a serious matter, and would have to be dealt with, but later. This weekend was for them, and they were both determined to make it as joyous as possible.

They were getting married on D-Day, June 6. Even after 60 plus years from that courageous day, the French never forgot. They still called the Americans their *liberateurs*. Giselle was especially touched by this anniversary, having survived four hard years of occupation as a young girl.

There were still a few stressful moments getting the renovations finished, but by June 5, miraculously, it was done. Suzie had arrived from the U.S bringing gifts. Her wedding present to them was an exquisite antique crystal decanter, perfect for the decantation of a bottle of Aumont *grand cru*. Her surprise gift came in a huge box. Punkin wondered how she had gotten it first on the plane from Georgia, and then on the train down from Paris.

When Punkin opened it, she laughed. Inside were blocks of Velveeta cheese, the glaringly yellow cheese that seems to have a shelf-life of a thousand years, cans of Rotel tomatoes, and of Wolfbrand chilli plus large sacks of tortilla chips. The wedding guests would sample Texas' famous appetizer, *chile con queso*.

The wedding weekend started on Friday with just the immediate family and Suzie going to the *Mairie*, mayor's office in Bordeaux, for the civil ceremony. Then the big church wedding and reception would follow on Saturday. A group of friends had already arrived from Paris and the Aumonts had installed them at the finest 5-star hotel in the area.

Punkin knew her future mother-in-law was watching her carefully. She was determined not to make any missteps over this weekend. She dressed very conservatively for the civil ceremony in a pale pink silk suit, her hair up in a chignon, and a small hat, also in pale pink with a tiny lace veil. This legal ceremony was done in French. Then the religious ceremony conducted by the Dean of the American Cathedral in Paris, would be done in English. Jean and Punkin had a surprise for their guests upon their arrival at chateau after the wedding in *St. Emilion*.

The "I do's" and the "bands" were signed in 15 minutes at the *Mairie*, and Punkin was officially Madame Aumont. The mayor kissed her on both cheeks, and Madeleine was beaming. She finally had a father and a mother.

They hurried back to the chateau where they were hosting a small cocktail for their out of town guests. The other friends of the Aumonts from Bordeaux would not come until the wedding reception on Saturday. This night, Punkin could relax and enjoy her Paris friends without being judged.

After the Thanksgiving fiasco in Paris when Marcel burst into her apartment, and made the violent scene, Punkin's American Club friends, Tom and Eleanor Charleson had dropped her from their social set. Tom had been injured tussling with Marcel and it took Eleanor a long time to forget. Eleanor had forced Punkin to pay Tom's doctor bills for his slight injuries and she felt she had no choice, although money was tight for her even then. But, time heals some wounds, all had been forgiven, and it was time to move on.

PARIS PERFECT

Eleanor was so impressed by Chateau Aumont. She felt little Punkin from Texas had moved up in the world. She wasn't going to miss this grand event. The Charlesons arrived from Paris with their dog, Clementine, and loads of luggage, the hotel staff told the Aumonts.

For the cocktail, Eleanor was dressed as usual head-to-toe in Chanel with the addition of some new, big diamonds, that Tom had given her on their wedding anniversary just two weeks before.

It was old home week for the Charlesons, Suzie and Punkin. They had so many grand times together playing heated rounds of bridge at the Charleson's sumptuous apartment on Blvd St. Germain.

They had been Punkin's first friends in Paris.

They had all gathered in the great room of the chateau with its walk-in stone fireplace, tapestries, velvet sofas and a variety of porcelains, Louis XV furniture and antique clocks. It was a grandiose room of over 50 feet long. After everyone had been offered their first glass of champagne, Eleanor took the blushing bride aside and said,

"I never thought you would land such a catch! Jean Aumont always seemed the perpetual bachelor."

"It just took our Texas girl to turn his head," Suzie said, overhearing the conversation, and holding a huge glass of champagne.

The weather this Friday evening was superb. It was predicted to stay sunny and cool for the whole weekend. It would be the perfect weather for the perfect wedding.

Damien Hunter had also arrived from Paris with his dog Choo Choo. It was only the second time Punkin had seen him in a suit, the first being the *vernissage* of his work at the American Club before the Thanksgiving holidays. This old college sweetheart of Punkin's had been the first artist to see talent in Madeleine. He offered to give her art lessons, and then used his influence to get her a place at the *Ecole des Beaux Arts*.

Also in the Paris house party was the Dean of the American Cathedral, Charles Huntington. He was having a grand time drinking too much champagne and eating the delicious *canapés*. The American Cathedral and the American Club's protégé program for wayward girls was how Punkin met her now official daughter.

Even the *grandes dames* of *President Wilson*, Adele de la Fontaine and Estelle Jonville had come from Paris. Adele was a long-time friend of Giselle Aumont's. They had known each other as girls in the convent school in Paris during the war. Giselle was so pleased that the two older ladies could attend the weekend festivities. It was grand for her to have some contemporaries in this much younger group.

Darling George Castellane, Punkin's lawyer and confidante, rounded out the Paris group. George was entertaining all with fascinating stories of his criminal cases. George didn't know that Punkin and Jean might have to enlist his services to deal with Marcel.

Two of the Birthday Club girls from Houston, Kathy and Janey, came without their husbands. This core group of 5 women had been friends since they were five years old, but her friends were much more conservative than she. They made a constant effort not to talk about politics or lifestyle.

With just the core group here this evening, Punkin thought it a good time to unveil her wedding present to Jean. It was the portrait she had commissioned Damien to do. The portrait he had done the year before of Madeleine was now hanging along the grand stairway among the other portraits of Aumont ancestors.

Punkin clinked her glass to get the group's attention.

"*Mes chers amies et famille*, I have a surprise for my wonderful new husband on this first day of our marriage."

With that announcement, she pulled the bell cord next to the fireplace to signal Loic to bring in the surprise. Damien had placed the portrait on a rolling easel covered in a silk cloth. With much flourish, Punkin pulled off the cloth and there she was immortalized in all her beauty.

As with Madeleine, Damien had captured her features perfectly. He had placed her in a dark green velvet gown to match her vibrant green eyes and accentuate her shiny blonde hair. Around her neck were her mother's lustrous pearls which she had since given to her new daughter. The portraits of mother and daughter would hang side by side on the staircase.

"Ok, Jean, now it is your turn to be captured on canvas," Damien said.

"Oh no, I can not compete with my two beautiful girls."

Jean looked at the portrait and then back at Punkin. He would tell her when they were alone, he knew in his soul he had made the right choice. He would live with Punkin and Madeleine contentedly the rest of his life.

The party continued longer than expected with the champagne and Aumont *grand cru*, flowing in abundance. The guests finally returned to the hotel around 10pm. Jean, Punkin, Madeleine and Giselle, *la famille Aumont*, were exhausted but exhilarated. All of them would have trouble sleeping this night. The wonderful news was that Jean and Punkin would finally be able to share the same room.

The foursome climbed the big staircase together, turned off the grand chandeliers, and kissed each other *bonne nuit*. The formal wedding would take place tomorrow at high noon in the church in *St. Emilion*.

CHAPTER 17

I Do.... Again

Even though Jean and Punkin were legally man and wife in the eyes of the French government, she still wanted to hold to the superstition that the groom should not see the bride in her wedding dress before she walked down the aisle. Punkin had no idea where her father was, as he had left her and Big Punkin years before for a younger woman. Walking her down the aisle would be dear George Castellane.

Finally, able to sleep in the same room, the couple consummated their new marriage finding inventive ways to be quiet in the throes of passion. Their normally raucous lovemaking was tuned down a bit, and when they both came, they covered each other's mouths with a guilty laugh.

At dawn, Punkin went to Madeleine's room where she would try to sleep a few more hours and then change into her wedding attire. She felt a little bloated from all the eating and drinking the night before, but she slid perfectly into her satin sheath. Madeline zipped up the back of her dress carefully, and then they put on her veil. Giselle had come into Madeleine's room to bring in the prized family heirloom.

Punkin had been right about choosing the dark red silk dresses for the bridesmaids. The red showed off her daughter's blue eyes and dark hair to great effect. She would not see Suzie in her dress until they got to the church, but Suzie was such a stunner, she was sure she would look perfect. The Birthday Club girls from Houston, Kathy and Janey, would be in the house party, and hand out bags of rice at the church.

Punkin had stuck to her superstition and had not seen Jean all morning. Neither of them could go through this morning without talking, so they called each other several times on the house phones. In a grand estate like the Aumont chateau, there was a switchboard of numbers for the bedrooms, kitchen, dining room, stables and outer wine buildings, including Loic's cottage on the grounds. He was helping the newly married Aumonts with the reception surprise for their guests.

At eleven o'clock, the cars arrived to take the family to the church, about 30 minutes away.

St. Emilion, in Punkin's opinion, was one of the few charming towns in the Bordeaux region. The other towns were kind of dull, with most of the land in the region being taken up by the grand wine estates. *St. Emilion* still had remnants of Roman times. The little church looked like something out of a storybook. It was surrounded by the Roman ramparts of the town and was a small stone building covered in ivy. At the entrance of the church were rows and rows of rose bushes, in shades of pink, peach, white and red.

The cars arrived at the church promptly at 11:30 for the 12-noon service. As they got out of the car, a wind gust caught Punkin's long veil and swept it up like a parachute. It took both Giselle and Madeleine to hold it down until they got inside. Like those stories of Jane Austen's about country life, the townspeople of little *St. Emilion* were all gathered along the walk way of the church to get a glimpse of this prosperous local couple. Punkin thought if Bordeaux had "paparazzi", they would all be there with flashbulbs popping.

When they entered the church, most of the guests were already seated. Kathy and Janey were standing in the entry with their bags of rice at the ready. Punkin kissed them hello and spotted Suzie looking gorgeous indeed in her bridesmaid dress. She hugged her and they both teared up a bit.

Since Jean had no brothers, standing up with him at the altar were Tom Charleson and Jean's boyhood friend, Antoine de Polignac.

Punkin had just met Antoine, and learned he was single. He was a gorgeous guy, as tall as Jean, with dark hair greying at the temples. He had hazel eyes the color of agate. She must seat him next to Suzie at the wedding dinner. He could be Suzie's "Mr. Darcy".

The wedding party had just enough time to arrange their outfits and get Giselle seated in the front row before the wedding march started. George was at Punkin's side.

"Are you ready Madame Aumont?"

George smiled at her and gently took her arm.

Madame Aumont she was, at last. Although already legally married the day before, she was again the bride and all eyes would be on her. After a half-century of life, she was marrying her Prince Charming. As they walked down the aisle proceeded by Suzie and Madeleine, Punkin stared straight ahead gazing into Jean's eyes. That was all she saw. Everything else around her in the church was a blur. She swore she saw a light radiating around Jean's head.

Dean Huntington preformed the usual Episcopal service with the bride and groom taking communion. They exchanged rings that Jean had especially made for them. The wide bands of gold were both engraved inside with "J&P". The service was over in less than 1 hour. Jean and Punkie hurried down the aisle to much applause and back out into a waiting car. They disappeared so fast, no one, including Giselle and Madeleine, had any idea where they had gone. They assumed it was back to the chateau to change for the reception and dinner.

It took the wedding guests and wedding party of 100 people another thirty minutes to get back to the estate. As everyone filed into the great room, there was still no sign of the happy couple.

"*Mamie*, where are *papa et maman* ?"

Madeleine looked a little concerned.

"*Je ne sais pas, ma chere*. I am sure they are still changing. Go up to their room and see," said Giselle.

The wedding guests were enjoying champagne and gourmet *hors d'oeuvres* in the living room. They had not even noticed the bride and groom were not there. The French doors were open to the expansive terrace that looked over the vineyard. Because it was such a pretty day, many of the *invitees*, were taking their drinks and appetizers out to the terrace. Madeleine came back downstairs and met her grand-mother in the entry still greeting arriving guests.

"They are not in their room. Where could they be?"

At that moment, they heard laughter and applause coming from the living room. Giselle and Madeleine hurried into the room to see what all the commotion was about. From the terrace, all eyes were on Jean and Punkin, coming up from the rows of vines at a quick gallop on their horses Chiquita and Stormy. Punkin had changed into a white satin riding jacket, white jodhpurs and white riding boots. Jean was attired in his jodhpurs with black boots and a black tuxedo jacket. Punkin's long blonde hair was flying in the wind.

They pulled their horses to a stop at the entrance of the terrace. Chiquita and Stormy reared up into a greeting for the guests. Each had a bouquet of flowers tied to their bridles. Maurice and little Babette, also decked out for the occasion in small top hat and veil, arrived behind the horses, panting to keep up.

"*Les Aumonts sont arrivee*"

Punkin and Jean said simultaneously with big grins. What a treat for all. Only Loic had been in on the surprise. Punkin and Jean dismounted and Loic took the horses. The couple joined their guests on the terrace.

"Is that how they do it in Texas?"

Suzie said to the couple, handing each of them a glass of champagne.

"Well that is a little odd, I must say."

Eleanor Charleson, said. She was always a stickler for social etiquette.

Punkin felt very comfortable in her riding clothes. The satin jacket made the outfit just dressy enough to carry her through the evening. Her boots were much more comfortable than her wedding heels.

What a happy day!

CHAPTER 18

Le Diner de Marriage
The Wedding Dinner

Punkin and Jean both began circulating among their guests, always keeping each other in eye shot. Since Punkin was in such a good mood, she decided to jump right in and tackle the *grandes dames* of Bordeaux and their husbands. She did not know any of them, but they were easy to pick out in the crowd. This group, who hung tight with their own kind, was huddled together in one corner of the living room, eyeing the other invited guests from the "big city" of Paris. As she approached them, the husbands beamed at her approach- the wives didn't.

Most of the women were older than Punkin. They seemed not as old as Giselle, but close. They were all immaculately dressed, but in a very old fashioned style. There was lots of Chantilly lace around their necks, long strands of pearls and of course longer hemlines than the younger crowd. Their hair was coiffed close to their heads. They all looked like they were wearing grey helmets.

Antoine de Polignac was standing with them and since Punkin had met him, he might break the ice for her with the others. She walked up to his side.

"*Bonsoir Antoine*", Punkin smiled

"*Re-bonjour Madame Punkin*"

Antoine smiled back, but with a little reserve. He began the introductions.

Of course, he made all the introductions in French. Punkin was glad she had not drunk too much yet so she could concentrate. She met Monsieur and Madame "de" something from Margaux, Monsieur and Madame something else from Pauillac and Monsieur and Madame de Saint Cyr from the vineyard adjacent to the Aumonts. She must for sure remember their names.

As the conversation continued, all were curious how an American had ever married a member of their tribe. You could tell they were thinking how she had come to live in their midst, and what were they to do with her. They were very polite, said the wedding was lovely, and that it was so *drole*, funny, the way Jean and Punkin had arrived at the reception. Punkin could sense they did not think her satin riding habit was appropriate for dinner. The wives all said she must come visit their chateaux while the "men folk" were working the vineyards. Punkin shuddered at this thought.

After spending what seemed an eternity with these people, she caught Jean's eye, and motioned him to meet her in the grand hall. To get away from the tribe, she explained that she and Jean needed to confer about the dinner which was about to be served. A corner of the vineyard, closest to the house, had been tented, and would be the venue for the seated dinner of 5 courses with accompanying wines.

"Hello husband", Punkin said as she kissed Jean on the cheek.

"Hello *ma femme*. How are you getting on with our neighbors?"

"Ok, I guess, except I realize I have got to enhance my French skills. Your neighbors have a strong local accent, and speak French like they are still living in the 19th century."

Jean laughed and hugged his girl.

"Not to change the subject, but I think the dinner is almost ready. We probably should call everyone *a table,*" said Jean.

"Good idea, and I want to make sure that at our head table, Antoine sits next to Suzie."

"You matchmaker," said Jean

Hand in hand, the two, glowing from the day, went into the living room to stand by the massive fireplace. They clicked their glasses to get everyone's attention.

"*Mes chers amis, messieurs et madames.* Thank you all for coming and sharing this joyous occasion with us. *Diner est maintenant servi au terrace.* Take your drinks and follow the candles to the dinner tent," said Jean

The dinner tent was colored a pale pink, with a large chandelier hanging from the middle of the ceiling. The tables were festooned with large vases of pink and white roses. Giselle had brought out her best *Havilland* china and old French silver. The crystal wine goblets sparkled in the light of the chandelier. Adding more of a pink glow were hundreds of votive candles along the walkway to the tent, and long white taper candles on each of the 10 tables in silver candelabra. A dance floor of parquet was set up in the middle of the tent, with the tables surrounding it. A DJ would provide music for dancing after dinner. This would be a long, French dinner which might last until dawn. Vive la France!

Toasts, toasts and more toasts were made to the feted couple. Dean Huntington, standing to make his toast after much champagne and wine, lost his balance and almost fell face first into his dessert. The most moving tributes were from Madeleine and Giselle. Madeleine, as maid of honor, made the first.

"*Chere maman et papa.* I never believed two years ago, that such happiness would come into my life. Meeting *maman* and then discovering *papa* was a true miracle. *Sante et felicitaions a Monsieur et Madame Aumont* from their daughter Madeleine."

Madeleine emphasized the word daughter. She was slowly forgetting Marcel and the years of being shuttled from one family member to another. She said a silent prayer that Marcel would never find them again.

Giselle, overflowing with emotion from the wedding and the anniversary of the end of the war, could barely make her toast. Her voice was choked with tears.

"*Mon cher fils et* Punkin. The happiest days of my life until today were the day that Jean was born, and the end of the terrible occupation of my country. Today I welcome dearest Punkin and Madeleine as cherished additions to the Aumont family. May we all live together in blissful peace until the end of our days."

By midnight, the last course had been served and the dancing began. After dessert, the famed Bordeaux *marc*, made from the skins of the grapes and fermented for a long time, was served as a *digestif*, after dinner drink. This 100-proof golden liquid was dynamite, very similar to Normandy's famous *calvados*.

Punkin had asked the DJ to play some songs of the war years. The big band sounds of Tommy Dorsey and Glenn Miller, was music Punkin loved, too. Since this weekend was also the anniversary of D-Day, she wanted Giselle to have some of her music. She and Jean took the first traditional dance of bride and groom alone on the dance floor. Their favorite song was "The First Time Ever I Saw your Face" by Roberta Flack. All 100 sets of eyes were concentrated on the handsome couple. Jean, like Punkin, was a very good dancer, and as the song ended, he dipped her almost to the floor and planted a kiss on her lips. All cheered. The Aumonts took a bow.

Next was Jean's dance with Giselle. The tune this time was Glenn Miller's "Pennsylvania Station". The wedding guests were amazed to see Giselle "cut a rug" with a fast jitterbug. Jean was astonished, and he twirled and twirled her as she kept time perfectly to the beat. Another round of applause and *mere et fils* took a bow.

Family dances over and all fueled by the champagne, wines, *marc* and great food, the wedding guests crowded the small dance floor. Punkin was so amused to see staid Eleanor and Tom get on the floor to do the "twist" to an old 60's tune. Eleanor even kicked off her shoes!

When the DJ cranked up the Rolling Stones, everyone was gyrating like mad. It was so interesting to watch the different styles of dancing between the French and the Americans. Everyone was in such a *convivial* mood, even their staid Bordeaux neighbors. They began switching partners. Even Loic and the kitchen staff joined in. It wasn't Woodstock, but it was a love fest none the less.

By 2am, most of the guests had staggered home or gone back to the hotel. The Aumonts had reserved private cars for the out of town guests. The DJ finally gave up the ghost at 3am. Punkin and Jean could have danced all night. The final song, so appropriate to wrap up the evening, was the great World World 2 song, "I'll be Seeing You". Jean, Punkin, and Madeleine joined together and danced entwined. Giselle, too "pooped to pop" sat watching them, a contented smile on her face.

Lights were out by 4am at Chateau Aumont. One more event was the wedding breakfast in the morning at the hotel, hosted by the Aumonts. The fantasy would turn into reality after this weekend. Punkin would start her new life as the wife of a famed *vigneron* of Bordeaux.

CHAPTER 19

Canicule- Heat Wave

The weather had been picture perfect for the wedding. June was usually a very cool month in Bordeaux. France rarely had extremely hot weather even in July and August. The two weeks after the wedding, all were busy opening wedding presents, and sending thank you notes. Madeleine had her first lesson with her new art teacher in town, and she seemed to like him. She had been such a good sport to give up the *Ecole* temporarily and live in Bordeaux.

The chateau which was massive, seemed bright and airy and easy to get around. Punkin actually loved the stairs to the first and second floors. It gave her great exercise running up and down them. She and Jean were also riding everyday. There was so much wonderful land to explore on the Aumont estate. It covered over 100 acres.

Punkin was learning how to be the *doyenne*, lady of the house, from Giselle. There were daily lunch and dinner menus to plan, party invitations to answer, and preparations for the *vendage*, harvest in September. Giselle reluctantly handed over her grandiose set of keys to all the closets, doors, silver and china cabinets. There must have been over 20 keys on a long gold chain that Giselle usually wore on her *Hermes* belt. It seemed Punkin was now the "queen bee".

By the third week of June, the weather changed. A major heat wave, what the French call a *canicule*, descended over the whole country. The temperatures hovered around 100 for several days. Of course, the chateau did not have air conditioning. The heat was putting everyone on edge, especially our Punkin. She decided to address the issue of putting in central air at least in the bedrooms of the chateau. This conversation with Giselle did not go well.

"*Gigi*, I was thinking, since we have access to a marvellous renovation crew who did a grand job on the new wing, they might give us an estimate to put central air conditioning in the bedrooms. It is so hard to sleep at night in this heat."

Giselle, who always looked cool no matter what the weather, stared at Punkin like she had two heads.

"Air conditioning? Why would we want air conditioning? It is not healthy for the body."

Uh oh, here we go again with the old ways. As the conversation continued, Giselle said not only did she not want to put central air in the bedrooms but she advised Punkin to keep all the windows shut to keep out the air. Punkin thought Giselle's old age was making her demented. With 100-degree heat, and 80 percent humidity, the family needed air circulation.

Punkin then suggested fans, but Giselle said they were no good either. This "fear" of fresh air, Punkin discovered, was rampant in the French. She and Giselle made some courtesy calls on their neighbors, whose houses were shut up like a tomb. Punkin almost fainted at one of the visits. She was served hot tea in a stifling dining room, and wanted to throw her tea cup through the window to break the glass and get a little air in there!

This air conditioning thing became a *cause celebre* for Punkin. She figured this would be her first chance to exert her power as lady of the house. She was hopeful that Jean would agree. After many discussions and some heated arguments in their hot bedroom at night, he didn't agree. He sided with his mother. That was a shock to Punkin, but she knew when she made the decision to move to Bordeaux, life would not be a piece of cake.

She decided she and Madeleine needed to take a little trip back to Paris for the week. The Aumonts were newlyweds, but a little distance after these first few weeks, might be good for both of them. Plus, the girls would not stay in the stifling *pied a terre* of Jean's. Punkin would use some of the Aumont money that was now hers, too, to put them in a first-class hotel with the coldest AC she could find. Madeline could see her teacher, Monsieur Abadie at the *Ecole*, and Punkin could meet with George and see what they might be able to do to put Marcel away for good. They would leave the next morning.

CHAPTER 20

A Week in Paris

After much cajoling and sweet talking, "Jean's girls" convinced him they had to go to Paris for a week. Jean insisted that the Aumont's chauffeur, Joseph, drive them, but since they would not need a car while in Paris, they would train home on the TGV.

Punkin checked them into a suite at the George V on *avenue George V*, and upon arrival in their spacious rooms, she turned the AC to an icy 68 degrees. She still couldn't get cool from the *canicule* week. Even Joseph was hesitant to turn on the car AC on their trip into the Capital. What was it with the French and fresh air? Punkin was amazed how resilient the French were in the heat.

Suzie, Punkin's sidekick, was back in the U.S. and she really didn't want to spend time with stuffy Eleanor although she really liked Tom. Punkin and Madeleine would invite them to dinner one night and that would be it for their social obligation to the Charlesons. Punkin felt a little lonely without Suzie, but she had her little girl with her, and the *soldes*, sales, had just started so they could have fun shopping and picking up some bargains.

Madeleine immediately called Professor Abadie. She wanted to get over to the *Ecole* as soon as possible to discuss which of her art he was going to display in the exhibition coming up in two months She also wanted to show him her latest work, a portrait of her *grande-mere* Giselle. It was a marvelous portrait that captured Giselle's elegance and beauty. She was still a stunning woman at age 82.

They got settled and went for lunch to their favorite *bistro*, the Atlas, near their old apartment on *rue st. peres*. Pasquale, their waiter, greeted them warmly. They ordered their usual meal of *moules/frites*, steamed mussels with crisp French fries. The Atlas was only 2 blocks away from the *Ecole* on *rue Bonaparte*. Madeleine would spend the rest of the afternoon there.

Punkin was going to call George and hopefully see him the next day to discuss the Marcel situation.

"*Cherie*, after you have your meeting, perhaps tonight we can go to the *Hotel Raphael*, and have dinner on their roof top terrace. Would you enjoy that?"

"I would love it. You can see all of Paris from the roof top garden. You are so close to the *Arc*; you feel you could reach out and touch it!"

They planned to meet back at the hotel around 6pm, change for dinner, and then make a night of it at the *Raphael*.

CHAPTER 21

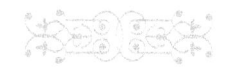

Madeleine In Trouble

"Fame is a vapour, popularity an accident, and riches take wing. Only one thing endures and that is character" Horace Greeley

Madeleine hurried off to the *Ecole*. She ran into her fellow classmates, Sophie and Antoine, and it was a grand reunion. Antoine's work would be in the exhibition but sadly, Sophie's would not. Madeleine had forgotten how fragile and destitute Sophie looked. Her summer cotton dress was threadbare. The skin on her face had broken out in an angry red rash, probably caused by the stifling heat in her 6th floor walk-up. Professor Abadie was also happy to see her. He approved of her portrait of Giselle and it indeed would go in the show. Wouldn't Giselle be proud!

By the time Madeleine had visited with everyone, it was already 6pm when she told her mother she would be back at the hotel. The *George V* was a good 20 minutes away by metro, and in rush hour the trains would be packed. She hurried out the main entrance not paying attention to anything around her. As she stepped out on *rue Bonaparte*, she came face to face with Marcel. He was standing so close, she felt she could not breathe.

"You *stupide putaine*, I knew you couldn't stay away from your precious art school. I have been here waiting for you every day for weeks. Now I have you!"

Marcel grabbed her arm and almost lifted her off the sidewalk as he pushed her down the street. Madeleine's heart was pounding.

She was so terrified she thought she was going to be sick. It might be good to throw up *moules/frites* all over Marcel. She tried to scream, but couldn't. Marcel guided her down into the metro.

"I have a little surprise for you back at our home in *St. Denis*. Several men are waiting there who have never had the pleasure of your services. They will take turns on you and I will watch."

The metro car was crowded. The two were crammed up against sweaty people trying to get home. The car jerked as they left the *rue de bac* station, and Madeleine bumped hard up against Marcel. She could feel his switchblade in its sheath attached to his belt. Other passengers boarded the train at *Chatelet*, and Marcel and Madeleine were pushed farther into the corner of their metro car.

Another lurch, and Madeleine's hand was almost on the knife. Marcel was saying nothing, but still had a tight grip on her. Another 15 minutes on the metro, a lifetime. How was she going to get Marcel's knife? At *Bercy*, near the *Gare de Lyon*, on the direct route out to *St. Denis*, a group of rowdy footballers boarded the train. They were all drunk, and loud, pushing into the already over-crowded car. Here was Madeleine's chance.

Marcel was distracted by the footballers, and momentarily, he let go of his grip on her. She grabbed the knife and in one swift motion, plunged it into his stomach, twisting it hard to do the most damage. She had wanted to kill Marcel, and now she had.

Marcel's expression was one of surprise, then pain, and then he collapsed to the floor, blood coming out of his mouth, nose and the gaping wound. A girl standing next to Madeleine saw the blood, and shrieked in a high-pitched wail.

"*Au secours, au secours-* Help!"

Madeleine dropped the knife. Marcel lay dead, his eyes wind open. A thrill ran through her body. The bastard was dead, and she wasn't sorry.

The next minutes passed in slow motion, a blur of colors and noise. The train was stopped and the *gendarmes* arrived quickly. Madeleine couldn't focus. She saw the blue of the policemen's uniforms, and the rowdy crowd moving away from her as if she was a pariah. The pain of the handcuffs pinching into her wrists brought her back to reality. She was taken away in a patrol car to go the short distance to the city jail near *Hotel de Ville*.

In rapid succession, she was booked, asked if she wanted a lawyer and given one phone call. She wanted her mother. However, she would not be able to talk to Punkin. By French law, the suspect can't speak to anyone directly. The police procedure is to call the designated contact and explain the situation. She wanted her mother!

CHAPTER 22

It's Murder

> *"Character is not cut in marble—it is not something solid and unalterable. It is something living and changing, and may become diseased as our bodies do."* George Elliot

Punkin's phone rang and she did not recognize the number. It was already way past the time for her little girl to be back at the hotel. Punkin had paced a hole in the hotel carpet.

"Madame Aumont, *ici le commissariat de police*", a strong cold voice said.

"I understand French, but you can you please speak in English? Has something happened to my little girl?"

The policeman then explained in broken English the whole incident. Madeleine was being charged with murder. She would stay in the City Jail for 48 hours before being transferred to a women's prison outside Paris. He further explained that the only person who could visit her in the next 48 hours would be her attorney.

Punkin couldn't believe what she was hearing. She told the policeman that she would call the family attorney, George Castellane, immediately, and he would come to the jail later that evening. The policeman seemed to know George. Punkin thought that was a good sign.

She hung up the phone and dialed George's number.

Madeleine was put in a dreary cell, but thankfully by herself. The sun was still high in the sky. In the summer, it never set until

10pm. The sun made shadows on the bars of her small room with a cot, sink and pail for a toilet. She could only see part of the Paris sky. She would just have to be patient until George arrived. She was sure her father would come to Paris immediately. She thought of her poor grand-mother. Such a shock might do her real physical harm at her age.

Madeleine was a strong girl with a good character. If she had survived the dismal years of her childhood and living with Marcel, she would survive this, too. He was dead, out of their lives, and she just needed to convince a jury that it was self defense. She decided that no matter what George Castellane suggested, she would tell the whole sordid truth again about her life, but this time to a bunch of strangers.

By 8:30pm, George had arrived at the jail. He was allowed to see Madeleine but only for a 30-minute consultation- also French law. They were seated across a table in a windowless room painted that pucky green of hospital corridors. There was a strong smell of bleach.

"Madeleine, what have you told the police?"

"Not much. I told them the truth that Marcel had kidnapped me, and I had no choice but to try to escape."

"That is all well and good, but the prosecutors will say there was no need to kill him," George continued.

"But I had to kill him, so he would be out of our lives for good."

Madeleine could see the strained look on George's face.

"Madeleine, I will say this quickly since we do not have much time. Never say that to anyone else! If we are going to get you free, we must establish that you killed Marcel in self-defence because he was going to kill you."

Madeleine was shaking and George reached out to touch her hand.

"You are in for a pretty long haul. I will not be able to apply for bail for you for 6 months. Your parents can visit you once you get to the prison. I can't give you much more encouragement except to say, we may have a good case since Marcel has a record with the police and is known to be a petty criminal and pimp. Your parent's standing in France might also help."

Before anything else could be said, the matron took Madeleine away.

There was no longer a death penalty or the *guillotine* in France, but murder was the most serious business. George rushed off to the hotel to talk to Punkin.

CHAPTER 23

The Defense Strategy Begins

George arrived at Punkin's hotel around 10pm, and Jean Aumont arrived at midnight. He found Punkin and George sitting in the living room in deep discussion. He embraced his wife and then said to George.

"*Mon dieu*, George, this is the most nightmarish situation. Punkin tells me you are one of the best criminal attorneys in Paris. I hope you are the best to get our little girl out of this mess."

"I do not want to lie to you Jean. I have been telling Punkin this is a tough situation. I saw the police report and talked to *les gendarmes* who arrested Madeleine. There are several witnesses who were standing close to Madeleine and Marcel on the train. They clearly saw her stab him."

"What does Madeleine say? It is inexcusable that we can not even visit our child!"

"I know *cher ami*, but you know French law is tough. She seems to be not contrite at all. She said she is glad she did it."

Jean crumpled into a chair, his face ashen.

"Well what is our defense going to be? We can't let this ruin her young life."

"We are in luck in one way. Marcel does have a record and the police know that he was already arrested twice for threatening both Punkin and Madeleine, first at the Thanksgiving lunch, and then when he cut Punkin's hand down at the Taborette. I just wish Punkin had made formal charges against him then."

"I am sorry about that, too, George. I was in shock and hurt badly, and just wanted to get to the hospital. But I did keep his letter."

George looked surprised. He had forgotten.

"What letter?"

"Before we moved away to Bordeaux to mainly get away from Marcel, Madeleine and I received the vilest letter from Marcel at *rue st. peres*. How he found our address I do not know. Remember, I sent you a copy."

Jean looked disgusted, remembering the letter himself.

"Might that help, George?"

"Anything we can do to dig a bigger hole for that bastard Marcel, the better," said George, and continued.

"We will try to keep Madeleine's background before she became an Aumont to a minimum, but your little girl is determined to tell her whole desperate past to a jury. I will try to convince her that honesty is not always the best policy."

"What is our next step?" Punkin and Jean almost said in unison.

"The first step in this long process is the case will go to an investigating judge who will be assigned to look into this matter. He will interview all pertinent parties, the police and Madeleine. He will look at the autopsy report, and try to track down any relatives of Marcel's.

Sorry, but this process can take 2 years before we go to actual trial.

But take heart. I will use all my influence at the *Palais de Justice* to get Madeline released into your custody. The bad news is she will not be allowed to leave the prison for 6 months. You will have to put up a pretty heavy bond, as well."

"I don't care if it is millions of euros. There is nothing I will not do for our daughter," said Jean, his face contorted with fear and determination.

"Hold that thought. The judge will probably ask for 500,000 euros, and once Madeleine is back in Bordeaux, she will have to regularly visit the police there every two weeks until the trial date is set.

There are two levels of murder in France: *assinat*, which is premeditated, and *meurtre* which is like in the US, a manslaughter charge, without premeditation. We will of course go for the second charge since after talking to Madeleine, I believe her that it was in self defense."

"How are we going to break the news to Giselle?" Punkin queried the two.

"*Maman* is tough. She survived the war, she can certainly get through this," said Jean.

"Your mother might even be a good character witness. I do not want to put either of you on the stand, if I can help it. Juries love old people. They believe them."

They continued talking until dawn. Jean and Punkin went back to his *pied a terre* to try to sleep. Both knew it would be a long night. Since it was so late, they would call Giselle first thing in the morning. Jean had called her as he arrived in the city, and reassured her then, that there was nothing to worry about. Punkin felt a deep ache all over her body. She yearned to touch her child.

A heavy fog and rain had started on this early morning in late June. It made everything look dull and dead.

CHAPTER 24

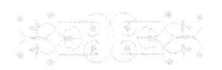

The Accusations Start

Jean and Punkin had fallen in bed exhausted. When morning came, the accusations started. Jean looked at Punkin lying beside him, and began to talk non-stop.

"Remember I TOLD YOU, before we were married, when you finally told me about Marcel and his continued threats we would have to do something sooner than later- Well now it is LATER and I pray it is not too late! If we are going to have any chance to save our child, no more secrets! I am going to get up, fix some café and then figure out how to tell *maman* this ugly story. We had over 100 years of peace in the Aumont family and then you came along."

Punkin tried to calm her husband down but to no avail. He would not even look her in the eye. He went into the other room out of ear-shot to call his mother. She could not hear what Jean was saying, but felt so sympathetic. Poor Giselle. She agreed with Jean on one thing. She hoped this news would not kill her mother-in-law.

Punkin was trembling, and still half-asleep. She felt at that moment, she had been nothing but trouble to the people she loved most in the world. Maybe she just needed to disappear and get out of all of their lives.

To Be Continued . . .

ABOUT THE AUTHOR

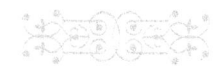

June Rives has been in love with France since she first visited at age 16. She moved from Texas to Paris in 2000, involving herself in the ex-pat community. She has held positions as Welcome Committee Chair for the American Cathedral, and Board member of the American Club of Paris.

June is the author of "Merci, Monsieur..A Guide for Living in la Belle France", a how to navigate the French system as an ex-pat. Paris Perfect is her first fiction novel.

After 15 years in Paris, June now divides her time between her hometown of Houston, Texas, and Paris. She is the owner of two businesses which specialize in vacation rentals in France and travel itineraries to France and Italy for the American market. In addition, she guides wine tours of the Burgundy and Bordeaux Regions.

June is fluent in French, and conversant in Italian and Russian.

CPSIA information can be obtained
at www.ICGtesting.com
Printed in the USA
BVHW07s0854171018
530416BV00003B/349/P